The Accused

Nancy Rue

PUBLISHING
Colorado Springs, Colorado

THE ACCUSED
Copyright © 1995 by Nancy N. Rue
All rights reserved. International copyright secured.

Library of Congress Cataloging-in-Publication Data
Rue, Nancy N.
    The accused / Nancy N. Rue.
      p.   cm. — (Christian heritage series ; 4)
    Summary: Josiah and Hope, two young Puritans living in Salem Village in 1691,
find themselves caught in a bitter feud between the Putnam and Nurse families.
    ISBN 1-56179-398-1
    [1. Puritans—Fiction.   2. Christian life—Fiction.   3. Vendetta—Fiction.
4. Massachusetts—History—Colonial period, 1600–1775—Fiction.]   I. Title.
II. Series: Rue, Nancy N. Christian heritage series ; bk. 4.
PZ7.R88515Ac   1995
[Fic.]—dc20   95-10950
                                                CIP
                                                AC

Published by Focus on the Family Publishing,
Colorado Springs, Colorado 80995
Distributed in the U.S.A. and Canada by Word Books, Dallas, Texas

Editor: Gloria Kempton
Cover Design: Bradley Lind
Cover Illustration: Jeff Haynie

Printed in the United States of America

95 96 97 98 99/10 9 8 7 6 5 4 3 2 1

For my sister Phyllis—lover of all kids

Josiah Hutchinson stared at the fringe of icicles that hung from the roof outside the window. There was nothing he hated worse than being stuck inside on a winter day. Now, if he could be out *in* it—ice-skating on the Ipswich River or sledding down Thorndike Hill— *that* would be different.

Josiah heaved a sigh that rose from the pit of his misery.

"I don't see what could be the matter with you," his sister, Hope, said, darting her eyes up from the wool she was carding. "You go out almost every day to school while I'm caged in here like a prisoner, churning your butter, pressing your cheese—" she stopped and waved a tuft of wool at him, "—carding your wool."

Josiah waved the spool he held in his hand at her in return. "Aye. I go to school every day and I'm stuck inside *there.*"

Hope gave her dark curls a toss. "Ha! And on the way, you throw snowballs and chase chipmunks and climb trees."

Josiah's blue eyes went wide and innocent, but Hope rolled her own black ones at her younger brother. "And don't try to lie to me, Josiah Hutchinson, because you can't do it." She reached up and hooked the wire teeth of her wool card in his sandy curls.

"Hey!"

"Hey yourself!" she cried as she tugged.

"What goes on here?"

Everything came to a halt. The wool card slithered back to the wool and the yarn skittered back to the spool. Two heads, one black and one blonde, bent over their jobs with the fervor of bees. Their father was in the kitchen.

"And is this the way a thirteen-year-old girl and an eleven-year-old boy behave when left to their own devices?" he asked.

Hope looked at her broad-shouldered father as if she hadn't the vaguest clue to what he was referring. But Josiah kept his eyes down and his fingers racing. You didn't fool Joseph Hutchinson, although Hope was always willing to try.

"Ach!" Papa said. "If your brother wants his hair woven into my stockings, so be it. Josiah!"

This time Josiah's head popped up. "Aye, sir?"

His father looked at him with his piercing blue eyes, hooded by bushy, sandy eyebrows. "Both Rebecca and Francis Nurse are ill, and their children are hard put to continue providing for them, what with their own farms and children to care for. There are few others who will help them—with the whole village following after the Putnams, and the Putnams hatin' the Nurses . . ."

His father's voice trailed off, and Josiah finished the sentence in his mind. *And us. The Putnams hate us.*

Papa cleared his throat. "I've a mind to send over a load of firewood to help them."

Josiah saw the scowl forming on Hope's face, even as he felt the smile creeping onto his own. They both knew what was coming.

"Fetch the small sled from the barn, load it with cut wood, and tie it on," Papa said. "See you get it over to the Nurse farm before dinnertime."

Hope's eyes flashed. *Dinnertime!* That was over an hour away. As well as Josiah knew every fold and ridge of Essex County, he'd have the job done in fifteen minutes and would spend the rest of the time playing in the snow. She knew it, and Josiah knew she knew it. He tried not to look too triumphant as he reached for his jacket and hat.

"Good day, Hope!" he said over his shoulder as he slipped out the kitchen door.

She turned and glared and waved a threatening wool card in his direction.

Hope doesn't really hate me, Josiah thought as his heavy leather boots squeaked in the snow on his way to the barn. At one time he thought she did. But over the past months, they'd shared enough adventures and discoveries to make them more friends than little brother and older sister. But in the everyday chore of being a Puritan child in 1691, it was easy to become jealous of what small freedoms the other was allowed.

Personally, Josiah thought Hope had it good. She could stay warm at those times when he was out in the bone-freezing night chopping wood. She got to hang around the kitchen all day, where she picked up all kinds of interesting information from Papa and Mama's whispered conversations. And Josiah always thought Papa was just a little easier on Hope—just a little slower to shoot her a glowering look that would melt a stone, just a little less quick to assume she had yet again put the family in some fix.

Josiah shook his head as he dragged the sled across the gleaming, hard-packed snow. But that was all changing, just since last spring when he had helped save Hope's life. And last summer when he had rescued her after everyone thought she was a thief. And last fall when he had found his runaway cousin.

Besides, he would rather be Josiah Hutchinson than anybody else right now, because he was out of the smoky kitchen, with rolling fields of snow and an hour of free time stretching in front of him—something that almost never happened.

It had snowed all day the day before, which meant that the paths connecting the farms of Salem Village were buried under knee-deep drifts. Josiah plowed through every one of them, kicking clean white clumps into the air and watching them scatter. The Nurse farm was south of the Hutchinsons', just across Crane Brook. In summer, most of the land between the two farms was marshy. But now all

Josiah could see was a wide-open field rimmed with bare trees that were etched against a blue sky so brilliant, it almost hurt his eyes to look at it. Ahead of him, a crow hopped across the top of the snow and curled its beak down against the cold. To Josiah, nothing had ever looked blacker. Another bird called out into the frosty air—maybe a sparrow or a chickadee or even a small hawk—screeching for hidden dinner. But mostly the snowy village was quiet. Josiah was a quiet person himself, and he liked the silence—and the freedom.

He would enjoy being by himself, he decided, until he dropped the wood off for Goody Nurse. Then, with the sled empty, perhaps he could pry Ezekiel Porter or William Proctor free to take on Thorndike Hill. Ezekiel was always bragging about how fast his sled was.

Josiah stopped suddenly, and the sled swerved behind him. A long row of fluffy pine trees stood just ahead of him, and one had just dumped a branch full of snow onto the ground. Something, or someone, was hiding behind the thick cone of green and white, and a chill went up Josiah's back. It was a chill not caused by the New England cold.

Sometimes a course of action just popped into Josiah's mind and he was doing it before he knew why. Now was one of those times. He flew across the field with the sled bouncing behind him before he even thought to ask the question.

A second later, he wished his mind had told him to take off the other way, back in the direction he'd come. For cutting out of the row of pine trees were four figures. Josiah would have known them anywhere, even if they hadn't hurled themselves right into his path.

He tightly grasped the sled's rope and swung to the right, just out of the reach of Eleazer Putnam, John Putnam's son. He was the same age as Josiah, though a head taller. But he was skinny and easy to get past.

"Idiot!" a voice behind Josiah cried out. It had to be Jonathon Putnam, the tall, wiry fourteen-year-old son of Nathaniel Putnam. He was the leader, and Josiah knew he was screaming at his cousin Eleazer for missing the chance to trip him.

Josiah pelted toward the Nurse farm, the sled full of wood still in tow. He dug his boots in harder, but the snow was becoming icier, and he knew he was running over the frozen marsh.

"Get him, Richard!" Jonathon shouted.

Suddenly, Thomas Putnam's son Richard slid across the snow on his belly with his arms outstretched and landed at Josiah's feet. Josiah leaped, and the runners of his sled bounced over the other boy. Richard cried out in pain, and Josiah would have stopped if he hadn't known Edward's son Silas, the last of the cousins, was gaining on him from behind.

The red clapboards of the Nurse house came into view as Josiah careened to the left. He had only a few strides of frozen marsh left and he could tear up the hill. He hadn't had many run-ins with Silas, but he was pretty sure he could outrun him. Just a few more steps . . .

But with his next footfall, Josiah's leather boot caught a patch of ice. Both feet flew straight out in front of him, and he came down squarely on his back on the hard snow. The sled veered out beside him and landed with a thud against his thigh.

Josiah closed his eyes as he gasped for some of the cold air. When he opened them, four pairs of eyes glared down at him out of four oversized Putnam heads with faces the color of holly berries. That was the thing about the Putnams, Josiah thought miserably. They all had the same big-headed, red-faced look about them. They all looked mean, and they were.

"Well, well, what have we here?" Jonathon said.

Josiah pulled himself up onto one elbow and followed Jonathon's gaze to the sled. The pile of wood was peppered with tiny clumps of snow, but it was still tied securely to the sled. Josiah tried to sit all the way up and grab for it, but two pairs of Putnam hands grabbed him from behind and dug their fingers into his shoulders.

Eleazer stood in front of him and smiled in a twisted way. "You won't be going anywhere soon unless we tell you," he said.

Jonathon hissed, and Josiah knew he thought that was funny. Hissing through his front teeth was the way Jonathon laughed.

"Where do you *want* to go, Josiah Hutchinson?" Jonathon asked.

"I *am* going to Francis Nurse's farm," Josiah said through his teeth, which were beginning to chatter.

If you wanted to stay warm in the New England cold, you had to keep yourself dry. Snow was seeping through Josiah's woolen breeches and spilling into his boots. But it wouldn't do for the Putnams to see his lips trembling. It wouldn't do for them to think for a minute that he was scared. Frightened people were their favorite targets.

Eleazer peered into Josiah's face. "My, my!" he said in a mocking voice. "Poor Master Hutchinson's lips are blue. Do we have anything to warm them up with?"

Jonathon hissed again. "Perhaps the girls can help us. Josiah likes girls, don't you, Josiah?"

All four heads twisted toward the pine trees, and Josiah's went with them. Below the lowest branches, he saw the bottoms of two skirts. Girlish giggles rang through the air.

"Which would you prefer?" Eleazer's mouth curled. "We have Abigail Williams and Ann Putnam."

Josiah stifled a groan. He had had his problems with both of them, and they were just as hateful and sneaky as the boys. Josiah's mind started to race. Boys he could usually shove out of the way or hurl some insult at. But girls were always harder for him to deal with.

"What's the matter, Josiah?" Richard buzzed in his ear. "I thought you loved girls."

Josiah clenched his teeth.

"Enough of that now," Jonathon said, his voice suddenly commanding. "Why are you going to the Nurse farm? They have naught to do with the village."

"They live here, same as you!" Josiah snapped.

"Aye, and think they're high and mighty, too!" Eleazer

said. "Francis Nurse is nothing but a tray maker, but he thinks himself a wealthy landowner."

Josiah had heard all of this before when the Putnam brothers—Thomas, Nathaniel, Edward, and John—had argued with his father. The Putnams believed that anyone who bettered himself was going against God's will. Papa believed it was right to use God's blessings to better provide for the family and the community. Francis Nurse had become a prosperous farmer, his father had told the Putnams, because he didn't spend time worrying about what other people had and arguing over whether they deserved it! Those kinds of arguments made the older Putnams hate Joseph Hutchinson as much as the younger ones did Josiah.

"Are you takin' them this firewood?" Jonathon demanded.

"Aye, I am." Josiah managed to pull his right shoulder out of Richard's grasp. "There's hard sickness in their house, and my father thought—"

"Of course there is," said a voice behind him.

Abigail Williams, Reverend Parris's niece, was picking her way importantly across the snow, her skirts lifted up to her knees. If her guardian, Reverend Parris, had seen that, Josiah knew he'd be crying to heaven for forgiveness for her.

She stopped and looked at Josiah through her narrow green eyes. "Of course there is hard sickness in the Nurses' house," she said in her tight little voice, "because they refuse to attend my uncle's church—just like the Hutchinsons. And they refuse to pay the taxes for his salary—just like the Hutchinsons. And they won't provide their share of his firewood—just like the Hutchinsons." She crossed her arms over her chest and smirked at Josiah. "It wasn't enough that you had sickness in your own house last spring and that your sister was left half deaf from it. You Hutchinsons still haven't learned—"

"Ah!" Eleazer said, waving both hands in the air as if he were flagging down a passing hawk.

"What is it?" Jonathon growled.

"I know what's to be done with this load of firewood."

"It's to go to the Nurses'!" Josiah cried.

"No!" Eleazer's big head was almost purple with excitement. "It's to go to Reverend Parris's."

"Aye!" Abigail cried.

The rest of the Putnams joined in, and Josiah even heard Ann shouting from the trees. Only Jonathon scowled, probably because it wasn't his idea.

"I'd rather set fire to him with it." Jonathon kicked his foot against Josiah's leg.

"Do that another time." Abigail had her hands on her hips as if the decision were now completely up to her. "I'm freezing to death in that parsonage because the wood is practically gone. An agreement was made between this society and my uncle before we came here that our firewood would be provided by the people of the church."

"We're not people of his church," Josiah said, trying to control his chattering teeth. "We go to the church in Salem Town because some people, like you Putnams, wouldn't vote my parents in as members. So why should we give you our firewood?"

There was a stunned silence. People still weren't used to Josiah Hutchinson speaking up for himself. For ten years, he had stuttered and stammered and kept silent, and it was still a surprise for people like the Putnams when he let fly with a stream of words.

Since no one seemed to have an answer, Jonathon reached down and yanked Josiah up by the arm. He was slender but surprisingly strong. Josiah dangled a few inches over the snow.

"Good, then!" Jonathon cried. "We shall take the firewood where it belongs, but not before we put *this*—" he gave Josiah a shake, "—where *it* belongs!"

A chorus of shouts erupted into the quiet of the snowy morning. Josiah shouted, too, and kicked and clawed and bit. But there were a good many more of them than there were of him. It took them only thirty seconds to bury him in the snow and disappear into the trees, cawing like satisfied hawks.

Chapter Two

By the time Josiah managed to dig himself out of his snowy grave, they were gone. He didn't even have to look to know that the sled full of wood had left with them.

Be back in an hour, his father had said. Josiah looked at the sun and then shivered, half from the cold and half from dread. More than an hour had gone by, and he hadn't delivered a stick of wood to the Nurses—and now he stood here, drenched and freezing.

He tried to brush the snow from his pants, but it was already frozen to the cloth, and it felt like the water that had oozed inside had formed ice patties on his legs as well. Josiah shook his head to get the snow out of his hair and the fears out of his head. No, he decided as he found his hat and shoved it miserably over his icy, sand-colored curls. He wasn't going home until he got the wood back—and he wasn't going to do that until he got out of this glacier of clothing.

Puffing out a cloud of frosty air, he looked around and thought. There was only one place to go when you were in trouble, and that was to a friend. He had two. Ezekiel would spend too much time howling at him and asking him questions. William Proctor was the only answer.

When Josiah finally saw the rock walls pushing out of the snow, he knew he was on the Proctors' property, and he found a way to run faster. His feet were numb inside his boots. He wasn't even sure they were in there anymore. They felt like dead stumps clumping the ground as he plodded past the snowy trees that lined the path to the house on both sides.

The Proctors' house also served as an inn for travelers on the Ipswich Road and for villagers or townspeople wanting a cup of cider and some talk. But on a snowed-in day like today, few people were wandering the countryside. *Few people but the Putnams and Abigail Williams,* Josiah thought wretchedly.

That thought, and the thought that he didn't want to have to answer any of William's father's questions, nudged Josiah to retreat behind one of the many boulders that dotted the Proctor farm behind the house. He pulled his wooden whistle from the pouch he kept tied around his waist. Then he blew the signal and listened to it echo through the winter air. He blew again, harder. Inside, with fires roaring and the diamond-shaped panes of the windows tightly closed, it would be hard to hear.

But within minutes, the back door opened and William Proctor's white-blonde, spiky hair poked out. He looked around timidly, the way William always did things, and then ran toward Josiah's rock. He was panting puffs of frosty air when he got there.

"What happened to you?" he cried when he saw Josiah.

"Shhh! Get down!"

William ducked behind the boulder and stared at Josiah, who looked like he was half snowman.

"I got into it with the Putnams," Josiah explained under his breath. William leaned in close, his pale blue eyes wide as he listened. "They took the sled full of firewood I was supposed to take to the Nurses."

"What do they want with firewood?" William asked. "Are they just being mean?"

"Aye, but I'm sure they took it to Reverend Parris's. You know how he thinks everyone is supposed to supply it for him. Anyway . . ." Josiah took a deep breath and hugged himself with his stiff-cold arms. "I have to go and get it back, but I can't do it in these clothes. I'll freeze to death!"

"Aye. You can borrow some of mine. And there's no one around. It's safe to come in."

Josiah grinned at him. If William said it was safe, it was safe. He wasn't known for taking chances.

When they reached William and Sarah's room on the second floor, William pulled out a pair of breeches, a shirt, and a pair of woolen stockings and laid them across Sarah's bed.

"You ought to come with me," Josiah said as he changed

into William's clothes. "I could get the wood loaded onto the sled so much faster with you there."

William's eyes grew even wider, but Josiah could see the draw of excitement in them. William was cautious, but he liked nothing better than an adventure, as long as someone else did the planning.

"We'll go back by Fair Maid's Hill," Josiah said, "so we won't run into the Putnams again. It'll take longer but—"

"Shhh!" William hissed.

Josiah listened and heard heavy footsteps on the stairs. He snatched his wet clothes and pulled them under Sarah's bed with him. If it was John Proctor, Josiah didn't want to be found. Mr. Proctor was an even bigger man than Papa and quicker to grab the switch when children weren't exactly following the rules.

William slipped out the door and met his father at the top of the stairs. From under the bed, Josiah couldn't hear what they were saying, but John Proctor didn't sound as if he were praising William for some job well done. In a minute, his heavy boots clomped back down the stairs, and William's followed. Then the front door closed.

Josiah scrambled out from under the bed and ran to the window to look out. John Proctor trudged across the snow toward his horse, and William tripped along after him. Quickly, he turned and looked up at the window. When he saw Josiah, he stole a glance at his father's back, then motioned wildly to Josiah to get out—fast. Josiah heard John Proctor bark at his son without turning around, and William plunged after him through the snow.

His hands shaking, Josiah rolled his wet clothes into a ball and stuffed them under William's bed. Then, carrying his jacket, he crept silently down the stairs and down the back hall that led to the back door. Quickly shaking the snow off his jacket, he put it back on and then charged toward Fair Maid's Hill. It would have been so much easier, and even a little bit fun, with William along. But if he had to do it himself, he had to do it himself.

The parsonage where the Reverend Samuel Parris lived with his sickly wife; his daughter, Betty; and his all-too-healthy orphaned niece, Abigail Williams, was just down the road from the Hutchinson farm. But today Josiah took the long way. He didn't want to pass his own house and risk bumping into his father, or risk meeting any of the Putnams.

Although his breath came out in icy clouds as he ran, he wasn't cold. Dry clothes and fast legs did a lot for keeping a person warm. And a little fear, too. For as sure as he was that the wood and the sled were at the parsonage, he wasn't so certain that once he found them, it would be so easy to take them away.

Josiah slowed down when he reached the road that ran past the Hutchinsons' farm, the Meeting House, and the parsonage. It was noon. In fact, Mama would be putting dinner on the table and looking out the kitchen window, wondering where he was. With any luck, the Parris family would be inside having their noon meal, too. Josiah shuddered a little. Sitting around their table was probably a somber affair. He wasn't sure Reverend Parris had ever laughed in his life.

The training ground, where Sergeant Thomas Putnam trained the village militiamen in case of Indian attack, quietly rested under a blanket of snow. Josiah grinned as he hurried past it and slipped into the trees that bordered the Parris property on the back side. His father had often said it was ridiculous to think that the Indians who lived around the village would ever attack it. Josiah agreed. One of his best friends had been an Indian. And now he had another Indian friend—somewhere.

Josiah stopped and crouched behind a cluster of thick holly bushes behind the parsonage. He could hear a low-pitched woman's voice shouting something, but he had no idea what. She was talking in some other language.

Josiah strained to see through the leaves. There she was, on the back step leading into the Parris kitchen. Her dark face stood out starkly against the snow piled over the low doorway, and Josiah knew right away this must be Reverend Parris's slave from Barbados. He'd never seen her before, but he'd often heard Hope complain that Abigail and Betty never had to do any chores because their servants did them all. Maybe if Abigail had more to do, she wouldn't have time to run around making trouble for Hope and Josiah.

Even as Josiah peered between the thin branches, he saw the person at whom the woman was yelling, scurrying across the snowy yard toward the house, her skirts bouncing above her ankles. It was Abigail, and she obviously knew what the servant was saying, and it scared her. Josiah had never seen her jump at anyone's words, including her uncle's. No one told Abigail Williams what to do, even though she was only thirteen and an orphan. But now she meekly followed her uncle's slave into the house and closed the door behind her.

Everyone was probably in the house now. Josiah imagined them all sitting at the table in front of the fire, watching Reverend Parris to see if he would take a whip to Abigail or just stare coldly at her through the meal for being late to dinner. Josiah pushed aside the thought that he was going to miss his own dinner, and he crawled out from behind the holly bushes.

There wasn't much to the Parris property. The village was supposed to provide most of their food, so they didn't need a large farm like the Hutchinsons and Porters had. The sled and the wood should be easy to find, if they were here yet.

Josiah suddenly remembered that Abigail had been part of the wood-stealing caper, so she must have been showing the Putnams where to put the wood when she was called to dinner. He quickly found her tracks in the snow and followed them backward. Her hurried trail led him right to the woodshed—and right to the sled.

He could see why Abigail had almost missed the midday meal. They had unloaded the wood and stacked it in a sloppy pile next to the sled. He imagined Abigail standing over the Putnam cousins, hands on her hips, telling them how to place every piece. Josiah smirked. If he ever stacked wood like that, his father would make him do it over again.

But there was no time to gloat. His father would do worse than that if he didn't get home soon.

Josiah quickly picked up two pieces of the firewood and placed them on the sled. Before he had loaded even half of the pile, his upper lip was beaded with sweat, and he was wishing more than ever that William had come with him. The sled would have been loaded and they would have been halfway home.

He picked up two more pieces. He would just have to work fast and then tie it as best he could. It really wasn't that far to go.

He stopped and frowned as he looked around the shed. Where was the rope, anyway? It would be hard to get it as far as his house without something to tie the wood onto the sled. What had they done with the rope?

Abandoning the sled for a minute, Josiah crept around the tiny woodshed. There was no window and only the light that sneaked in through the crack around the door to see by. He squinted into the darkness and felt his way around. When the door flew open, it slapped him to the ground.

"What you do, boy?" said a voice like gravel.

Josiah looked up into the angry face of a very dark man.

‡ ⁙ ‡

Chapter Three

"**W**hat you do?" the black man asked again. "You steal?"

"No!" was all Josiah could say. He usually didn't say much anyway, and it was almost impossible to get out more than that when staring into the face of this man.

He was taller than anyone Josiah knew, and his skin was as black as the inside of the woodshed. Josiah would barely have seen him at all, were it not for the glint in his black eyes. They, and the hair that strung down to his shoulders, were even blacker than Hope's and Mama's.

But the thing that froze Josiah to the ground was the look on the man's face. His lips were pulled apart to reveal a scattering of yellow teeth, and his gleaming eyes were aimed at Josiah like twin muskets. It would not have surprised him if the man had whipped out the knife he carried on his belt and plunged it right into him.

Is this the devil? Josiah thought wildly. *Have I met the devil?*

"You come inside," the man said roughly. He hoisted Josiah over his shoulder like he was fetching a bag of cornmeal. "You come see Master."

It was when they were almost to the parsonage that Josiah realized who this was. He had to be John Indian, Reverend Parris's other servant from Barbados. Josiah's heart was hammering too hard for him to do much of anything, but part of him wanted to knee the man right in the chest. John Indian had caused a lot of trouble for the Hutchinsons last fall. Hope had once told Josiah that he wasn't really an Indian, that he had just chosen that as his last name. Josiah was glad. This bandit wasn't worthy of any of the Indians he had known.

When they reached the kitchen, John Indian dumped Josiah to the floor. For the second time that day, eyes stared coldly at him as he lay helpless on the ground. The black woman, Reverend Parris, Mrs. Parris, Abigail, a pale, wispy girl he guessed was Betty, and Thomas Putnam. It couldn't be a more bullying group if it were the Putnam boys themselves.

Reverend Parris was the first to break the surprised silence. "What have we here, Indian?" he cried in his high-pitched voice.

"Found in woodshed," John Indian growled. "Stealing wood."

"The gall!" Thomas Putnam shouted.

Josiah winced. Couldn't the Putnams ever speak without

yelling? Even in the minister's house?

"Is it not enough that your father refuses to provide his minister with wood?" Thomas Putnam went on. "But you Hutchinsons have to steal it from him as well?"

"Does your father know you are here?" Reverend Parris asked as he hurried over to Josiah. He squatted down as if to better extract the truth from him.

"Of course he does!" Thomas Putnam cried before Josiah could even open his mouth. "He sent him, I'm sure of it!"

Josiah bit his lip. Puritan children were taught to speak only when spoken to by adults. Usually quiet, Josiah didn't have trouble doing that—except when people were spouting lies.

"Is that true?" Samuel Parris asked.

"No, sir!" Josiah pulled himself up to a sitting position, and Reverend Parris drew back as if to avoid some dreaded disease Josiah might have.

"Then, tell us what you were doing in the minister's woodshed!" Thomas Putnam demanded. He was standing up now, so that he towered over Josiah. His big head was the color of a giant radish.

I wonder why Reverend Parris doesn't ask the questions, Josiah thought. *It's his house, not Thomas Putnam's.* His father always said Reverend Parris was ruled by the Putnams, and Josiah could believe it.

"Answer me, boy!" Thomas Putnam screamed. "Has your father taught you no respect for your elders?"

"Aye, sir. I was—I was—" Josiah stopped and took a breath.

"Speak!" Thomas Putnam looked ready to burst into flames.

"Give him time, Mr. Putnam," Abigail said. "He's somewhat stupid."

Josiah's mouth cracked open like an egg. "I was taking back the firewood that was taken from me earlier today!" he said without a stammer. "I was on my way with it to the Nurse farm when—"

He stopped—not to keep from stuttering but to decide what to say next. Somewhere a little voice inside warned him not to mention the Putnams—not now—not under Reverend Parris's roof with Thomas Putnam breathing down on him.

"Well?" Thomas Putnam prodded. "What happened? You say it was taken from you? By whom? Indians?"

His big face suddenly lit up, almost as if he were pleased, and Josiah held back a smirk. Nothing would make Thomas Putnam happier than to have a reason to go after the quiet Salem Village Indians.

"No, not Indians," Josiah said, relishing every word. The happy glow faded from Mr. Putnam's face.

"I should like to ask a question," Reverend Parris said.

Mr. Putnam bowed his head graciously. "Certainly."

Certainly, Josiah thought. *This is his house!*

"Why did you come here looking for it?" the minister asked.

"Because he's a Hutchinson!" Thomas Putnam cried. "They've naught to do but try to destroy all that we are trying to accomplish in this village, Reverend." He began to

pace as if he were in a courtroom. All eyes watched him.
"They are not yet worthy to be covenanted members of
your holy church, because those of us who are members
have seen no sign of their complete faith in God. Nay, they
and their friends—the Porters, the Proctors, the Nurses,
my own half brother, Joseph Putnam—insist on gathering
in more and more wealth for themselves instead of trusting in the Lord and living off the land He has blessed us
with. Instead of showing themselves to be sincere in their
desire to join with us, they turn the other way. They refuse
to pay the taxes that pay your salary. They will not help to
provide food and firewood for this family we see gathered
around this table. They go so far as to attend a church in
Salem Town—the very place we hope to break away from
so this village can have its own government and be independent of the town's tyranny. In fact—" Thomas slammed
his palm down on the table for effect, causing the boat-
shaped trenchers to jump and clatter, "—they work against
our fight for independence. They make friends and do business with Salem Town merchants and seamen like Phillip
English. What's more . . ." he leaned in and lowered his
voice to a harsh whisper, ". . . they fancy themselves as
educated people, sending their boys to be taught by my
greedy half brother, reading books other than the Lord's
own Word, believing in the very things that will tear this
society apart!"

He let his last words ring in the air, and his arm sus-
pend there, too, as his audience soaked it all in. Josiah
nearly snorted with disgust.

Not a word of it was true, he knew. It had all been twisted and turned until it was nothing but an ugly knot. Last spring when the membership of the new Church of Christ in Salem Village was voted on, his mother and father had given some of the most moving testimonies of their faith in all of Essex County. But the current members were the Putnams and their friends, and they had voted that the Hutchinsons, Proctors, Nurses, and Porters should not be allowed to become covenanted members and take communion and vote in matters of concern. His father, angry that he was still expected to pay the taxes for the minister's salary, had decided to take his family to church in Salem Town, a long five miles away. They were accepted as members there and went as often as they could. It was a long trip, and now with the snow on the ground, it was almost impossible to get there.

Josiah scowled at the two men, who looked at each other with superior smiles. His father was every bit as godly as these men. More so. Papa always said a person should use the gifts God gave him, and God had given Papa a good mind. He was putting it to use to expand God's blessings. He had a prosperous farm and part ownership in a successful sawmill that allowed him to trade with shipowner Phillip English. He read books. The Bible was one of them, but he learned every night from the other volumes of history, science, and religion that were stacked next to his chair in the kitchen. He was a man his friends respected, and he wanted Josiah to be the same. He had sent him to school in Salem Town last summer, even though everyone considered Josiah to be slow and stupid. He had returned home able to read and write rings around Ezekiel and William. Now all three of them went to Joseph Putnam's school, and Josiah was far ahead of his two friends. There was no sin in that, his father had told him. Papa was a wise man. He knew the village wasn't ready to be independent of the town—because of all the quarreling and bickering among people like the Putnams and even the minister.

Suddenly, Josiah began to shiver. It was drafty and damp in this kitchen, and he wasn't given time to shake the loose snow off his clothes and boots before he was dragged in. The melting snow was seeping through William's breeches, and Josiah was miserable.

To his surprise, a pair of black hands took hold of his arms and pulled him up. The woman servant led him to the fire.

"What are you doing, Tituba?" Reverend Parris barked at her.

"This boy cold," she said.

Josiah looked at her sharply. The voice she used now was honey-soft and quiet. Not like the squawking one she'd used to call Abigail in.

Reverend Parris gave a pinched nod and turned to Mr. Putnam. They bowed their heads together and whispered. Tituba pulled a blanket from the settle and wrapped it around Josiah. When she turned to pour hot water in a mug, Mrs. Parris scraped her chair back from the table.

"Thank you, Tituba," she said in a voice as thin as a spider web. "I shall have my tea upstairs. Will you bring more wood for my fire, please?"

"Aye, mum," Tituba said in her low voice.

But as soon as Mrs. Parris was out of the room, she slipped the first mug of tea into Josiah's hand. "You drink," she murmured.

"Aunt said to get her some tea," Abigail said snippily.

Tituba picked up a tray and held it out to her. "You take, Abby," she said.

"I'll take it."

The tiny voice had come from Betty Parris. She climbed down carefully from her chair and stuck two sticklike arms out for the tray.

Tituba scowled at Abigail. "She too little. You take." She smiled at Betty. "You go. Talk to Mama."

With her lip thrust out like a hard bench, Abigail yanked the tray from Tituba and stomped toward the door. Betty trailed after her, and Josiah watched her go. Everything about her made him think of a trusting baby bird about to tumble from the nest, unaware there was danger below.

As if she felt Josiah's eyes on her, Betty turned at the doorway and looked at him. He could feel his cheeks turning scarlet. Girls always made him feel like a second thumb. But Betty smiled a pale smile.

Reverend Parris looked up sharply. "Get you gone now, Betty." But his voice was soft, and Josiah thought he even caught the shadow of a smile in his eyes as he looked at his daughter.

Like a tiny ghost, she did leave, and Reverend Parris shifted his gaze to Josiah.

"I have a mind to let him go, Thomas," he said. "He's harmless, I think, and I want no more trouble with Joseph Hutchinson."

Thomas Putnam glowered at Josiah. "Harmless? I think not. Wherever there is trouble in this village, it seems we find this boy as well."

Josiah knew what he was thinking. The gold chain last summer. The wolf traps last fall. Josiah had been there, but it was always the Putnams who made the trouble. The problem was, Reverend Parris didn't know that. He just listened to the Putnams.

"Nevertheless," Reverend Parris said, "I see no need to cause more trouble." He narrowed his eyes at Josiah, just the way Abigail always did. "I have stolen no wood, boy, so the wood in the woodshed belongs to me. You must be mistaken if you think any of it was taken from you. Now, be on your way—and stay away from my property."

Josiah swallowed hard. He could leave and at least the whole thing would be over. But when he got home, there would be his father to deal with. He didn't like to disappoint him. He'd come so far in his father's eyes. Besides, Reverend Parris did have one thing that didn't belong to him. But to speak up here, with Thomas Putnam . . .

"Well," Mr. Putnam said impatiently. "Will you be gone or shall I drag you to your father myself? I do not hesitate to do that."

"I will be gone." Josiah swallowed again, and then he tilted his chin up. "But first I must have my father's sled."

"Your father's sled!" Reverend Parris's voice wound up like a piece of twisted wire. "What do you mean?"

"It was taken from me today and it is in your woodshed."

Wild-eyed, Reverend Parris looked at Thomas Putnam, whose wide red face grew even redder.

"You talk nonsense, boy! If your sled is in Reverend Parris's woodshed, it is because you planted it there yourself!"

Josiah could barely keep from shouting back at him. The door came open then, and John Indian stepped into the room. Josiah had never known he'd left, just as he'd never heard him come to the woodshed. He had a way of creeping around that gave Josiah chills.

"Master," he said in his rocky voice.

"What is it?" Reverend Parris said, as if he were talking to an annoying fly.

"I find sled."

The minister's head snapped toward him. "A sled? Where?"

The tall black man pointed toward the corner of the Parris property furthest from the woodshed, just across from the Hutchinson farm. Then his terrible eyes locked onto Josiah, and Josiah choked back anything he was planning to say.

"Where is it now?" Mr. Putnam asked.

John Indian jerked his head toward the back door.

"Very well, then," Reverend Parris said to Josiah. "If it is indeed your sled, you may take it home. And see you don't bring it back here again with your schemes to blacken my name." His voice was winding up to the screech it always reached toward the end of his sermons.

Josiah slithered out the door. The blast of freezing fresh air hit him like a slap, but he didn't care. He snatched the sled rope off the ground and ran toward the Hutchinson farm.

Chapter Four

There was a time when Josiah would have kept his encounter with Reverend Parris and Thomas Putnam a secret from his father. Surely, Papa would think it was somehow his fault, that Josiah had once more brought shame on the Hutchinson family by getting caught being somewhere he wasn't supposed to be. But many things had happened since that time, things that made Josiah trust his father and made Papa trust him.

So, on that bright winter afternoon, Josiah stormed into the Hutchinson kitchen with his story ready. The sun was streaming through the diamond-shaped panes of the windows, bathing his family with yellow light as they sat around the table finishing up their salt pork and dried peas. It was so different from the dank, cold kitchen he had just left, and he stood for a minute, letting it warm him.

"Where have you been?" Papa said quietly. The quieter

his voice, the more trouble you were usually in, but Josiah marched straight to him.

"I've been in Reverend Parris's house, sir." And then he poured out the rest of the story, from the moment the Putnams stopped him in the field.

When he was finished, there was a silence in the kitchen. Everyone always waited for Papa to speak first. Mama was like Josiah; she seldom spoke at all. But Josiah knew Hope must be ready to burst. Her black eyes were snapping as she looked across the table at him. *She's ready to get the others and do battle with the Putnam boys,* he thought. The idea of adventure was splashed all over her face.

Papa finally chuckled softly, and the rest of them looked at him curiously.

"What do you find amusing in that story, Joseph?" Mama asked.

"Reverend Parris," he said. "Crying for his firewood. Allowing members of his church to send young boys out to steal it for him when his whining doesn't wheedle it out of the villagers." Papa shook his head. "Seventy years ago, my grandfather spent his first winter in Massachusetts in a crude hut in Plymouth. I'll wager he didn't cry half as much as Samuel Parris."

"Oh, Joseph," Mama said, her soft, dark eyes opened wide, "do you really think Reverend Parris knew those boys were going to steal?"

"Nay," Papa said. "Nor do I think Thomas Putnam himself knew it. I think those boys simply got lucky, don't you, Josiah?"

Josiah jumped. He wasn't used to Papa asking for his opinion. "Aye, sir," he said quickly.

"However," Papa went on, "I am certain the sons of Thomas, Nathaniel, Edward, and John Putnam get their ideas from their fathers. It isn't beneath the fathers to steal, lie, and cheat, so what can we expect from the sons, eh?"

Everyone muttered agreement, and there was another thoughtful silence.

Then Joseph Hutchinson looked at his children sternly. "This is a sign of the kind of bickering and arguing that is tearing this society down. They are wrong—the Putnams and their friends. But we are, too, if we allow ourselves to become involved in their senseless little 'war.' I will deal with this matter as I see fit. You will leave it to me."

He held their eyes—first Josiah's, then Hope's—with his own piercing blue ones. Josiah nodded obediently. He was a little disappointed, but what his father said was as firm as John Proctor's rock walls. There would be no arguing.

Josiah stole a glance at Hope, and he could see that she had other ideas. She said, "Aye, sir," in her clear, strong voice, but her eyes flashed as if she were angry.

She wants to do something, Josiah thought. And he groaned. That always meant trouble for him.

There was no chance that day to hear about the plans brewing in Hope's mind. There was dinner to clean up, horses to water, and wood to bring in. Papa took off in the wagon with another load of chopped logs for Francis and Rebecca Nurse, and as Josiah watched him go, he felt a

strange pang. Papa wouldn't have had to take time to do
that if Josiah hadn't let the Putnams catch him. Maybe
there was something he should do to make up for that.

But Papa had said no. And that was that. He stomped
his feet to get the circulation going again and peeked in
the window, where he could see Hope at her spinning
wheel. Maybe it was better that he didn't have a chance to
talk to her. This would give him more time to think of
ways to say no.

They had just finished their supper of baked apples and
bread that evening, and Papa had just lit his rushlight to
read from *Pilgrim's Progress,* when Josiah heard horses'
hooves galloping up the snowy road. He poked Hope. Ever
since her bout with the fever last spring, she didn't hear
well, so it was his job to let her know when something
interesting was about to happen. She used to have the
sharpest hearing in Essex County, and she hated being left
out of things because she couldn't hear well anymore.

"Company," she announced.

Papa closed his book on his fingers. "Who is it?"

Hope peered into the darkness at the lanterns. "Israel
Porter and Giles . . . John Proctor, Benjamin Porter . . .
and . . . Joseph Putnam."

Josiah made a dive for the door. His beloved teacher,
Joseph Putnam, had been away from Salem Village for several days, during which there had been no school. Josiah
missed him when he was gone—and now he was appear-
ing right at the front door.

Hope went immediately to the big fireplace and added a few more logs. Mama busied herself piling some corn cakes onto a plate and warming the cider. Papa welcomed his guests with his big arms open wide. Normally, he would have ushered them into the best room across the hall, and Hope, Josiah, and Mama would have stayed in the kitchen. But when it was so bitterly cold, much firewood could be saved if as many activities as possible took place in one room.

Benjamin Porter and his old, white-whiskered father sat on the settle, with Giles Porter standing behind his grandfather. Giles was Ezekiel's older cousin, a handsome young man who was always at Israel Porter's elbow. Some people said the old man was grooming him to someday reign as head of the Porter clan because he was smart. *And sneaky,* Josiah thought.

John Proctor pulled up a chair from the table to park beside Papa, and Josiah's thoughts jerked to the present. He was glad he had changed out of William's clothes and into his own. Mr. Proctor wasn't as understanding as Papa.

Joseph Putnam came to stand by Josiah and gave his shoulders a squeeze.

"What?" he said to him. "I'm gone only three days and you've grown in my absence. What are you feeding this boy, Deborah?"

Mama blushed at being spoken to, but Josiah knew she liked young Joseph Putnam. Everyone did. It was a frequent topic of conversation how such a good-spirited, handsome young man could come out of a clan like the Putnams.

Papa declared it was because Joseph had a different mother from the other four, and she had brought out the best in their father as well. When old Mr. Putnam died, he left most of his fortune to Joseph, which angered Thomas and his brothers. And when Joseph had married Israel Porter's granddaughter Constance, they nearly exploded in fury. That meant the Porters and Joseph Putnam stood to become by far the wealthiest people in the village. The Putnams were fast being shoved to the bottom of that list, because even Josiah's father was becoming more prosperous.

"What brings you here tonight, gentlemen?" Papa asked when the cider and cakes had been passed around and Joseph had shared his with Josiah.

Ezekiel's father, Benjamin, cleared his throat and looked around the room with his sharp Porter eyes. To Josiah, he looked just like Ezekiel, especially when he was about to share some complicated plan with the group.

"I was walking my northeast pasture today," Benjamin said, "and I discovered a newly built fence—one I certainly didn't put there myself!"

"Someone else built a fence on your property?" Papa asked.

"Aye—and it doesn't take much guessing to pinpoint who it was."

"Nathaniel Putnam," Papa said.

"Aye—and on your first guess, too, Joseph!" Old Israel Porter's eyes twinkled out of the web of wrinkles surrounding them. He was always making jokes, even in the most serious of times. He could surely make Papa smile, as he did now. Papa loved old Israel the way Josiah did Joseph Putnam. It was too bad, but there was something about the old man Josiah didn't always like . . .

"Did you go to him and confront him?" Papa asked.

"Aye, and Father went with me," Benjamin said.

"Of course Nathaniel denied doing it," Papa said.

"No, not in the least," Israel Porter said. "Admitted it right off, and said he had every right to do it."

"What?"

"Claims it's his property and he wanted to be sure Benjamin knew it, so he built a fence there to mark the boundary."

"But that is your land, is it not, Benjamin?" John Proctor asked, his eyes blazing. It was funny how John Proctor was so strong, like a warrior, and his children, William and Sarah, were as timid as little blonde mice.

"It is!" Israel Porter cried. "I gave it to Benjamin and Prudence when they were married!"

"Then, as I see it, there's a fence to be torn down!" John Proctor cried.

"Now, John, let us not be hasty," Papa said. "We must look at this thing from both of its sides and try to settle it peacefully. What say you, Porter?"

"Ach!" Goodman Proctor said. "Trying to talk peace to the Putnams is as useless as talking it with one of my cows."

"But it's up to Benjamin. What say you, my friend?"

Benjamin Porter looked at once at his old father.

I wonder if you will ever stop getting your answers from your papa? Josiah thought. Ezekiel's father surely hadn't.

Old Israel studied his gnarled hands for what seemed like a long time before he spoke. Then he looked at all of them with a smile. It was a smile Josiah never thought was quite real. It always looked to him as if it were drawn on with a quill pen.

"There are other ways to settle these disputes," he said in his well-mannered voice. "We needn't try to reason with the Putnams because, of course, as we know, they have no reason!"

He waited for the laughter, and it came, but it settled down quickly and everyone leaned forward. Everyone, Josiah noticed, except Joseph Putnam.

"And we needn't go to battle either. After all, we don't want to wipe out all of Joseph's relatives, do we?"

They pulled Joseph in with friendly smiles, and he nodded pleasantly at them. But Josiah knew when Joseph Putnam was truly happy—and when he was being polite. Right now, good manners smoothed his face, but happiness didn't.

"What are you suggesting, Israel?" John Proctor asked gruffly.

That was what Josiah wanted to know, too, and he perked up his ears. But it wasn't to be. Before old Israel could bring forth his wisdom, Papa suddenly looked at Josiah and Hope and said, "I think it's time you children were in bed, eh?"

It wasn't really a question but a statement that sent both of them scurrying up the stairs and into their frigid room. It was so cold there, their breath hung in the air as they undressed and Josiah climbed into his bed. Hope usually pulled her bed curtains tightly closed, but tonight she padded across the floor in her nightgown and nudged Josiah to move over. That meant she wanted to talk in secret and stay warm at the same time.

Josiah's stomach grew uneasy. "What is it?" he said, trying to sound irritable.

"You know what it is, Josiah Hutchinson!" she said. "We must decide what to do about this. There is real trouble in the village now—you heard it. If these kinds of arguments are going on, who's to say what's next?"

"'We' must decide?" Josiah said. "Who is 'we'?"

Hope sighed in disgust. "The Merry Band, of course."

Josiah sat up and glared at her. "Hope, no! Papa said it this afternoon—we are to let him handle it."

"Josiah, I am disappointed in you!"

Josiah flung himself back on the bed cushions. "Why?"

"Because." She folded her arms across her chest. "You have shown us all that you are not the brainless boy we once thought you were. And then you went off and learned to read and write and *proved* to us that you were not only bright in the ways of the world—you were actually smart in other ways as well. And *then* you came back here and showed amazing bravery and courage—" She broke off and leaned close to him, so that her nose almost touched his. "I do not see how you can shirk your responsibility to the Merry Band."

"What does that mean?" Josiah asked.

"That means we have all come to look up to you and

trust your decisions, even though you're practically the youngest, and now you're going to abandon the Merry Band—Sarah, Rachel, Ezekiel, William, and myself—just when we need you the most."

"Need me—to do what?" Josiah said carefully.

"To help our parents."

"Papa said he doesn't want us to help!"

Hope snapped her fingers in the air as if she were waiting for him to say that and she had caught him in the grave error of doing so. "What he said, Josiah Hutchinson, was that he would deal with this matter—the matter of the firewood that was to go to the Nurses—and we were to leave that to him." She wiggled her eyebrows wickedly. "He said nothing about getting back our firewood that is still sitting in the Parris's woodshed—or about this fence business."

"He didn't know about the fence then!" Josiah said in a loud whisper.

"Does that really matter?" Hope squeezed his arm with both hands before he could answer. "What matters is that we need you, brother. Without your wisdom, we can't accomplish anything." She let go of his arm and swung her legs out of the bed. "Let you pray about it, Josiah. I know God will tell you what's right."

She disappeared behind her bed curtains, and Josiah lay looking at the ceiling. *I surely hope so,* he thought as he started to pray.

He didn't have to have Hope tell him that going to God was the only way to figure out anything. He had learned

that the hard way. He waited until God felt close, and then
he started to talk to Him.

When he was finished, he could hear Hope breathing
evenly on the other side of her curtains, and he knew she
was sound asleep. But he lay awake for a long time, trying
to keep warm under his pile of quilts and thinking about
Joseph Putnam. He had been quiet tonight. He barely
joined in the conversation at all, and Josiah had a feeling
he wasn't happy about Israel Porter's "other ways" of solv-
ing things.

For that matter, neither was Josiah. Whenever Israel
Porter said that, and he seemed to say it often, Josiah
thought of a scene he'd witnessed last spring from the
top of a tree. He'd watched Giles Porter take apart one of
Thomas Putnam's fences and then put it back together
without its pegs so that Thomas's cows could easily knock
it down. When Josiah had gone down to investigate,
Thomas caught him and blamed him, although Papa hadn't
believed Josiah was guilty. But that wasn't what always
bothered Josiah. That wasn't why the scene came back to
his mind.

It was the fact that old Israel always *said* they shouldn't
lower themselves to playing tricks on the Putnams the
way the Putnams did on them. Yet, it looked to Josiah as if
he had his own sneaky little "ways" no one knew about.
Was it all right to do those things as long as no one found
out? Ezekiel Porter seemed to think so.

Josiah sighed and burrowed further under the quilts
until only his nose poked out into the cold. No matter

what Hope said, there would be no sneaky little ways for him. None.

Or so he hoped.

Chapter Five

"Well, gentlemen, I have a prediction."

William, Ezekiel, and Josiah all sat up straight in their seats. It was the first real sentence their usually talkative teacher had spoken all morning, and their ears were ready. It was deadly dull in the classroom when Joseph Putnam was quiet.

"Come over here. I want to show you something."

The three of them scrambled to the window of the room Joseph had had especially built in his new house for a schoolroom. If Salem Village wouldn't provide a school, as the government in Boston had told them they must, he would make sure they had one. Anyone could attend, but few sent their sons. Certainly, the Putnams wouldn't let Jonathon, Silas, Richard, and Eleazer be in the company of the likes of them. That was probably all right with Joseph, Josiah often thought. There would be more fights in the classroom than lessons if they were here.

As the boys gathered at the window and crowded for a view, Joseph nodded toward the sky. "Do you see those heavens?"

"Aye," they said in chorus.

"Nothing but a ceiling of gray. And do you see the ground below?"

Three heads nodded.

"Nothing but a floor of white."

He shook his head gravely, but there was a tiny twinkle in his eye.

"So, what's your prediction?" Ezekiel asked.

"Good question!" Joseph had told them many times that all questions were good. That was a rare attitude for a Puritan adult to have toward children, and these three took full advantage of it. "My prediction is that it is never going to stop snowing."

The boys hooted—with William looking at Ezekiel first to make sure it was indeed a joke.

"Next question!" Joseph said.

"What's to be done about it?" Josiah asked.

"Excellent question, Captain! And I have the answer." He crossed his arms over his chest and looked at them, eyes sparkling. "Since it is never going to stop snowing, and the snow will soon be up past the doors and climbing toward the roof, I think all three of you must be dismissed from school for the day. And—" he leaned forward and they bent toward him. His voice lowered to a whisper. "—I suggest you take time to play in the snow before you reach your homes because once you're inside, you may never get out again!" He wiggled his eyebrows and once more the boys howled.

Ezekiel and William were the first to throw on their jackets, hats, and scarves and dive for the classroom door.

"Come on, Josiah!" Ezekiel cried. "I brought my sled this morning. We can take Hawthorne's Hill!"

Josiah gnawed at the inside of his mouth before he answered. He really didn't want to take a sled right into Thomas Putnam's backyard—not after yesterday. But he didn't want to tell Ezekiel about his run-in with him, Reverend Parris, and the Putnam cousins either. Ezekiel was like Hope—ready to throw on armor and do battle on the spot.

"I'll be along later—maybe," Josiah said. "I want to stay and—and ask Joseph something."

Ezekiel put his mouth close to Josiah's ear. "Don't turn into a sissy schoolboy," he whispered. Then with a shrug, he was gone, with William in tow.

"You ought to go sledding, Captain." Joseph was picking up hornbooks and quill pens, and his voice seemed far away.

"Aye, but I wanted to talk to you."

Joseph turned and put the quill pens in their wooden box. He kept his back to Josiah longer than he needed, and Josiah began to squirm. Joseph Putnam was always there to answer questions, to help Josiah figure things out. But he seemed to be thinking about his own problems. By the time Joseph turned around to face him, Josiah had changed his mind.

"Perhaps you're right, sir," Josiah said. "I should go sledding. We can talk another time."

Joseph smiled, almost with relief, Josiah thought.

"Don't spend too much time at it," he said. "That really is a monster of a storm out there. We're in for a blizzard sure if this wind picks up at all. You'll get you home in good time, eh, Captain?"

He used his pet name for Josiah, which always made Josiah smile. Still, he felt a strange pang. Joseph was obviously eager for him to be gone. If he had one loyal friend in the world, Joseph was that person. It was lonely to stand right next to him and feel like he was so far away. Maybe if Joseph was troubled about something, Josiah could help, the way Joseph always helped him . . .

But Josiah discarded that thought as soon as it came into his mind. What wisdom could he possibly have that Joseph Putnam, his teacher, didn't already know?

"Good, then," Josiah said. "Tomorrow?"

"Aye, Captain," Joseph said. But he didn't smile.

It was snowing hard when Josiah left Joseph Putnam's house. He loved it when the flakes came down in silver shavings and ran down his face like freezing tears. But now that the sun was hidden by the snow, the cold bit and stung at his cheeks and shuddered through him. He wished he had a scarf, but he'd given his away last summer.

He decided to take a few minutes and skid across frozen Wolf Pits Meadow and then head for home. Joseph was right. If this kept up, there would be snow to shovel from the doorways before dinnertime.

In the summer, Wolf Pits Meadow was a marsh he could wade through to catch frogs. But in the dead of winter, it turned into a plate of ice, perfect for sliding across. Ezekiel had a pair of ice skates from Holland, but Josiah liked to get a running start and skid across on the soles of his leather boots.

Standing several yards back from the edge, Josiah leaned forward and went at the icy bog with his head bent low. He hit it squarely with his heels and then went down on his knees for a long slide, almost to the other side.

Perfect performance, he decided as he reached out and pushed a cattail. It shook off its cover of snow and stood there, brown and naked. And lonely.

Josiah got up and brushed himself off. He was pretty lonely himself. The quiet he usually liked when it snowed was more like an unfriendly silence today. His teeth were beginning to hurt from the cold, and pretty soon his feet and fingers would lose their feeling.

He turned to trudge toward the road that led to the Hutchinson farm when something caught his eye to the left, toward Beaver Dam.

Something blue.

Immediately, Josiah pointed his steps that way. The snow was falling in fast clumps now, but he peered through it and plowed on.

Something blue might mean a blue shawl. Pulled over the head of Wife of Wolf. He hadn't seen her in months and had almost decided she'd forgotten him.

He stopped suddenly, almost falling in the knee-deep snow, and fumbled with numb fingers for his whistle pouch. He put his whistle to his frozen lips and blew. It sounded like a musket blast in the snowy silence.

He strained to listen, and from the straggly stand of bare birch trees, a whistled answer came through.

"Wife of Wolf!" he called.

An Indian squaw, probably as old as his mother, emerged from the trees by the dam. She was wrapped in animal skins but still wearing the blue shawl. It was like the lantern of a friendly neighbor, and Josiah ran toward her.

"Wife of Wolf, where have you been?" he cried.

She didn't come to him, and as he got closer, Josiah saw that her wide face hadn't crackled into its thousands of tiny laughing wrinkles. Instead, he saw caution in her black eyes, and she put her finger to her lips.

Josiah slid to a stop beside her. "What is it?" he whispered.

Her eyes grew big, and she motioned with her hands in jerks and starts that Josiah knew must mean something. If the widow were still around, she'd be able to tell him what the Indian woman was saying. The widow was the only white person he'd ever known who took the time to learn things about the Indians. But she was gone—and what Wife of Wolf had to say was obviously important.

"What is it?" Josiah asked again. "Are you afraid?"

He knew she could understand him, just as his friend Oneko always had. She shook her head sharply and put her finger in the middle of Josiah's chest.

"*I* am afraid?" he said. "I'm not afraid!"

She bobbed her head up and down.

"I *should* be afraid?"

More head bobbing.

Josiah pulled his hat low over his forehead and looked around. "Why? Is there a wild animal? I'm not afraid of wolves, you know . . ."

She shook her head so hard, he was afraid it would fly off her shoulders.

"A person?" he said. "People?"

Solemnly, she nodded and put her hand around his arm. She pointed with a fur-covered finger.

"They're over there? But I must go that way to get home! Unless I go . . ."

He started to point toward Thorndike Hill, the long, hard way to the Hutchinson farm now that the shrill, wet wind was tossing the snow around in dizzying circles and whiting the world out.

But the squaw spun him around so that his feet made a spiral in the snow and his face was pointed toward Thomas Putnam's farm.

"I can't go that way . . ."

She pointed firmly in the direction of his own house and with a deep frown shook her head.

"The danger—the dangerous people are that way," Josiah said.

She nodded.

"So you want me to go that way—right into Thomas Putnam's arms!"

She nodded again.

Josiah felt like he was playing some ridiculous guessing game and losing fast.

"I'll just run home, fast as I can!" he said.

But Wife of Wolf was determined. She took hold of both of his arms from behind and began to push him. She was only about as tall as he was, but he was surprised at how strong she was. Since there was no point in doing anything else, he let her steer him—across the meadow, through the trees that lined its east side with their snow-laden branches, and into a crooked piece of land, just below Hawthorne's Hill.

Josiah thought he had been over every inch of Essex County—except for the lands owned by the Putnams. That must be where they were now. But before Josiah could protest, Wife of Wolf drove him to a large pile of snow. It turned out to be a tiny building, a building she knew about, because she pulled open its rickety door and with a gentle shove pushed him inside.

"Where are we?" he asked.

But there was no answer. Just like always, she'd gotten him to a safe place and then was gone. She had even closed the door behind her.

✢ ⋆✢⋆ ✢

Chapter Six

There were no windows. By the time Josiah got the door pushed open, the wind was swirling so madly, he couldn't see anything, including his own hand if he stuck it out at arm's length in front of him. Wife of Wolf had disappeared again, and the only thing to do in the blizzard that raged out there was to stay inside and wait it out.

Josiah brushed the thick layer of powdery snow off his clothes to stay dry and squinted in the darkness. This room was not even as big as the bedroom he shared with Hope, and it had no fireplace or furniture. With its dirt floors, it must have been a woodshed or storage cabin at one time.

It was sure no one had used it for a while. The door had groaned like a miserable old man both times it was opened, and there wasn't a scrap of anything around. Josiah slid down into a corner and pulled his jacket tighter around him. Of course, the squaw wouldn't have brought him to a place that was unsafe. If this shed was on Thomas Putnam's land, he surely wasn't using it.

Why did she do that? Josiah wondered. Why did the squaw always seem to appear out of the woods when he was in trouble and needed a friend, needed some help? He didn't know her by any name except Wife of Wolf, the nickname he'd given her himself. And he had surely never done anything for her.

Their only connection was the whistle she wore around her neck. It was the whistle he had given to his young Indian friend, Oneko, before the boy's father had assured Josiah and Hope in his frightening way that they would never see Oneko again. Josiah had discovered the squaw wearing it last fall—so she must know Oneko, must know where he was now.

Josiah gasped into the darkness. And she must be wearing it still. She had whistled back to him when he had signaled to her today. There had to be some way to find out who she was. Why she protected him. Whether she knew about Oneko.

A sound outside interrupted his thoughts. The wind was doing its own eerie whistling through the cracks in the little shed, but he heard something else—someone else—shouting above it, as if he were shouting to another person.

Josiah crept to the door and pressed his ear against the crack that ran around the opening. From somewhere in the midst of the blizzard, he heard them again—the voices.

They were so close, he could hear the words. So close, he could tell to whom they belonged.

"I tell you, he never came that way!" cried Eleazer Putnam over the wind.

"We stayed there forever! He didn't go home that way!" Silas's voice was grim, even though he was yelling.

"I saw him leave Joseph Putnam's!" came Jonathon's high-pitched voice. "You missed him, you idiots!"

"We didn't! He never came—"

"You are idiots!"

Josiah heard a thud as if someone had hit the snow, and he knew Jonathon had delivered one of his famous whacks to the side of one of his cousins' heads. The Putnams all did that. He had seen Nathaniel do it to Jonathon himself.

But Josiah also knew something else. It was he they were scouting around for, and at any minute they would certainly throw open the door of this shed and find him cowering here in a corner. It might not have been used for a while, but it probably belonged to Thomas Putnam nonetheless, and that meant another face-to-face meeting with the angry, red-faced man.

"Ouch!" a new voice cried from outside.

"Richard!" Jonathon called, ignoring his cousin's obvious pain. "Did you spot him?"

"I've cut myself. These wretched thorn bushes—they're the first thing to pop out of the snow!"

"I don't care about that. Did you find Hutchinson?" Jonathon was fairly screaming now.

Josiah cringed. With Richard out there, they would surely

come right to this shed of his father's and shove open the door. The only reason they hadn't done it up to now, he knew, was that they were right above it and couldn't see it. It was snowing so hard, its roof blended in with the ground. Only someone who knew it was here could find it. Like the squaw. Or its owner's son.

"I'm in pain!" Richard cried again.

"At least you can feel something!" Eleazer yelled to him. "I've lost my fingers—my feet—my ears!"

"You're all a bunch of sissies!" Jonathon screeched. Josiah could imagine his wide face beet red against the snow. "Do you want to find the wicked lad or not?"

"If he's out in this storm," Silas screamed back, "he's dead by now anyway, and we will be, too, if we don't get out of it."

There was a short silence—followed by a whack that resounded even over the wind.

"Ow!" Silas cried. "Don't hit me again, Jonathon. I won't have you hitting me anymore, d'y'hear?"

"I'll do as I please!" Jonathon shouted.

And their voices faded into the blizzard.

Josiah pressed his ear against the door and listened until he was sure they were gone for good. But even after he was sure, he waited—and waited—and waited. Through dinnertime. Through the howling of the wind and the mad swirling of the snow. Until his feet, his fingers, his ears, and his nose seemed to have fallen off. Only when he was sure that the storm was dying and the Putnam boys wouldn't return did he venture out and down the road to the Hutchinson farm.

Hope turned from the window and sighed with disgust because she couldn't see anything out of it anyway. It was nearly dark and it was still snowing.

"You're like a cat in a room full of leather boots, Hope," Mama said. "Sit you down and work at your needlework until it's time to fix supper, eh?"

Josiah watched her slump sullenly into her chair. No one got a worse case of cabin fever than Hope in the winter. He hoped his mother wouldn't leave the room before his boots dried and he could leave it himself to go outside again. Hope was surely more determined than ever to pump some excitement into their lives.

But his heart sank as Mama went to the peg by the door and took down her cloak. "I must see to some vegetables for supper," she said. "Mind you don't go out again today, Josiah."

With steps as soft as her voice, she slipped into the tiny room that Papa had built onto the back of the house for the storage of vegetables and salted meat just so Mama wouldn't have to venture into New England storms like this one. Josiah wished he hadn't. He wished the shed was a mile away so she would have had to send him.

"Where were you so long in the storm, Josiah?" Hope asked. She was already right next to him on the settle, and her mind was miles from the embroidery in her hand.

"I—"

"Don't try to lie to me. I know the Putnams were after you again, weren't they?"

Josiah sighed. "Aye."

"Don't you see that nothing is going to change unless we do something? Goodness—it isn't even safe to walk the streets of Salem Village anymore!"

"I wasn't exactly walking the streets. I was in Wolf Pits Meadow—"

"Where you have a perfect right to be!"

Something in her voice made Josiah look at her closely. She wasn't just craving adventure to get her out of this dull and stifling kitchen with its endless chores. She was angry—and Josiah even thought he saw some fear in her eyes.

"There's no need to be frightened," Josiah said.

"I am terrified!" she said. "For you! This is the second time in two days they have attacked you—or tried to. And they do it just for the reason Papa said—because they see their parents do it. So, while Papa and his friends fight their war, we must fight ours."

"No one has attacked Papa," Josiah said.

"Not yet." Hope let her needlework drop to her lap and folded her hands on top of it.

"What do you mean?" Josiah asked. "I can't imagine Thomas Putnam and Nathaniel, Edward, and John burying Papa in the snow!"

"No," Hope said, "but they'll find a way. They've already gotten to Benjamin Porter by trying to take his land. They've tried to get Papa before. They'll try again—in some devious way. And you, Josiah, have a responsibility—"

Josiah covered his ears with his hands.

"Listen to me!"

"No!" Josiah shouted. "Papa said no, and I'm saying no!"

"Foolish boy!" Hope picked up her needle and cloth and stomped to the other side of the room. She turned her back to him and was quiet. But her silence spoke like a stack of volumes.

It wasn't unusual to have visitors on winter evenings. The season was long and gloomy, and a pleasant chat with neighbors by the fire helped move it along.

But it was rare to have a visitor during a blizzard when a person could barely see to walk and the wind and snow tore through clothes and blistered bare skin.

When the heavy knocker on the front door clattered that night, the four Hutchinsons looked up from their reading and needlework and quizzed each other with their eyes. Papa walked grimly to the door. A knock on a night like this could mean only trouble. Josiah saw his mother's lips moving in prayer.

Within a minute, the door between the kitchen and the front hallway was opened again, and the doorway filled with the shoulders of John Indian. Hope perked up in her chair with interest, but Josiah shrank back on the settle and tried to look small.

But John Indian didn't look around. He hunched his shoulders as if he were uncomfortable and kept his eyes glued to the plank floor as Papa came in behind him.

"You say you have some message for me," Joseph Hutchinson said crisply.

John Indian grunted and stuck his hand inside his jacket.

Josiah caught his breath. Would he pull a knife on Papa?

But the black man presented Joseph Hutchinson with a rolled-up piece of parchment. Papa eyed him for a moment and then opened it. His deep-set blue eyes moved rapidly across the parchment and then they bored into John Indian.

"This is a receipt from Reverend Parris," he said. "For firewood!"

John Indian just grunted.

Papa thrust the paper into the servant's chest. "I gave him no firewood and I want no receipt. If he has wood of mine, it was stolen. I want my wood—not some useless document. Get you gone and tell him that!"

Josiah almost laughed. He was pretty sure John Indian couldn't say more than two of the words that had just sprayed so easily from his father's mouth.

But the laughter caught in his throat. For John Indian took the receipt Papa had pushed at him and angrily slapped it on the table.

"Message!" he said in his pile-of-stones voice. He jabbed his thumb at his own chest, turned on his heel, and stomped from the room.

Papa waited for the front door to slam before he picked up the paper from the table.

"Why did he do that, Joseph?" Mama asked timidly.

"Perhaps he knows that if he does not accomplish his commanded mission, he will be punished for it, eh?" Papa said.

Mama looked away as if she could feel the black man's pain. Personally, Josiah wasn't too worried about John

Indian's pain. He seemed to dish out enough of it to make it all come out even.

Beside him, Hope nudged him and he looked up. Papa had walked to the fire and was slowly burning the receipt until it was a pile of ashes. He returned to his chair, but he didn't pick up *Pilgrim's Progress* and continue reading. He sat with his eyes piercing the fire, and a brooding silence as cold as the winter that raged outside settled over the room.

Josiah shivered. But Hope looked at him with fire in her eyes. He could almost hear the words that burned in them. *Papa has been attacked, Josiah,* they said. *We cannot sit by and watch.*

Chapter Seven

It stopped snowing sometime during the night, and the sky was a brilliant blue by the time Josiah finished milking the cow and feeding the chickens. The kitchen was alive with light when he went in for breakfast, and Hope's eyes matched it. It wasn't long before Josiah learned why.

"I have already told your sister," Papa said to him as he stirred the hot porridge in his trencher. "I must spend the day at the sawmill, and with this much snow on the ground, there is little to be done around here. She is to be certain all is ready for dinner, and you are to be sure there is enough firewood in the house and the paths are shoveled. Then you are free to go sledding until dinnertime."

Papa wasn't like a lot of Puritan fathers. He knew that although children behaved on the surface like sober little adults who even dressed like their parents, they sometimes needed to shed their solemn faces and play. Josiah felt his face breaking into a grin, but he still had a question.

"What of school?" he asked.

"Joseph Putnam sent word," Papa said. "There will be no lessons today."

Josiah cocked his head, puzzled.

"Why?" Mama asked softly.

Papa gave her a look that Josiah knew meant, *I know, but I would rather tell you when the children are not about.*

Hope didn't miss it either. She gave Josiah a look of her own which read, *See?*

"Finish your breakfast, then, and be off with you," Papa said. "And—" he pointed a finger sternly at Josiah, "—see you are back here for dinner. You have missed it twice this week, eh?"

Not by my own choice, Josiah thought, but he said, "Aye, sir." He hadn't told Papa about yesterday's incident. No one knew about the squaw. He sighed heavily. Why did he always seem to have some secret buried inside him?

Hope kicked him under the table and nodded toward his trencher. *Eat!* her eyes said.

He did, and then he tore outside to bring in several armloads of wood. Within an hour, he had the pathways shoveled and the rope to the sled in his hand.

"I hope Rachel and Sarah are there," Hope said as they hauled the sled toward Thorndike Hill. "It will give us a chance to—"

"There they are!" Josiah pointed to Rachel, who was

wearing a bright red cloak that splashed against the background of white snow like cardinal feathers. Ezekiel was in a green jacket that flashed by them as his sled careened down the hillside. Behind him shot William Proctor, his spiky blonde hair sticking out like icicles under a blue knit cap. Josiah grinned. The Merry Band were colorful birds who'd left the nest for a few short hours to squawk and chirp however they wanted.

"Come on, Hope!" Sarah Proctor called from the top of the hill.

Hope didn't hear, and Josiah poked her. "Sarah is calling you. She wants you to share her sled because she's afraid to come down alone."

"Of course." Hope grinned, hiked up her skirts just above her boot toes and charged up the hill through the snow. She turned halfway up and waved her arms. "Come on, all of you! I have something to tell you!"

Josiah groaned. Why couldn't she just let them sled for today? Wouldn't tomorrow be soon enough for a crusade?

By the time Josiah reached them, Hope was already in the midst of her sermon and everyone was nodding except Sarah. She hung back quietly and looked down at the snow.

"So the Merry Band will strike again!" Rachel said when Hope was finished.

"Aye," Hope said.

"What will we do, then?" Ezekiel said. "You know, we could hide in the woods at the top of Hawthorne's. I'm excellent with a slingshot, and we could pelt those Putnams—"

"Shut it, Ezekiel," Rachel said.

It was her own way of whacking him on the side of the head, Josiah thought.

"We need a plan," Hope said.

"Must we plan out here?" Sarah's thin, pale lips were blue and trembling. "Can't we go to your barn like we usually do?"

Hope shook her head. "It's too close to home. Papa has given us leave to go sledding."

If we don't want Papa to know we're doing this, we shouldn't be doing it, Josiah thought.

"Where can we go, then?" Ezekiel asked.

I know exactly where we can go, Josiah thought. "That abandoned old shed where I spent the afternoon yesterday."

"What abandoned old shed?" Rachel demanded.

Josiah's head snapped up. He didn't know he had said it out loud, but he must have. Four pairs of eyes blinked at him, and four mouths hung open.

"It's—it's—well, I don't really know . . . ," Josiah stammered.

Rachel tightened her lips. "He's lying."

"What is it, Josiah?" Hope asked.

Josiah sighed. "It's an old woodshed or something that nobody uses anymore. It's at the bottom of Hawthorne's Hill, though. It might even belong to—"

"Let's go, then!" Ezekiel shouted.

And before Josiah could finish, they were hurtling toward Hawthorne's, their sleds bouncing along behind them.

"Come on, Josiah!" Hope called. "Show us where it is!"

All right, I'll show you, Josiah thought, pressing his lips together. *But I don't have to agree to anything else.*

The Merry Band oohed and aahed over the cabin as if it were a Boston mansion. Ezekiel built a tiny fire, and the six of them huddled around it. With the orange flames playing across their faces all shiny with cold and glowing with excitement, Josiah thought that the little shed wasn't such a bad place when it was filled with friends.

"Now, then," Hope began, "we can't let the Putnams believe they can attack us whenever they please. Or that any of their foolish tricks does one bit of good. Imagine Reverend Parris sending my father a receipt for firewood his friends stole from us!"

Rachel squinted her big Porter eyes over the sharp cheekbones that made her and all of her brothers and sisters and cousins look alike. "I bet Abigail had herself a good laugh over that one," she said.

"We can't let her laugh any longer. Now—" Hope looked carefully at Josiah, "—we made rules for ourselves last fall and we must follow them." She ticked them off on her fingers as the Merry Band nodded. "Nothing against the law. Nothing that will hurt anyone or damage property. And if questioned, we cannot lie."

Josiah squirmed in his spot between William and Ezekiel. He had made that last rule himself, but something about it bothered him. His father had never found out about their escapade with the wolf traps last fall because he had never asked. Somehow Josiah still felt like he had lied. Leaving out information was sort of like lying, wasn't it?

"As I see it," Hope went on, "there is only one thing to do—and that is to get back the firewood the Putnams stole from Josiah and put in Reverend Parris's woodshed. It wouldn't be stealing because it belongs to us. And it certainly wouldn't hurt anyone."

"I don't know . . . ," said Sarah.

While the others, except for Josiah, bobbed their heads in agreement, Sarah's face was puckered with doubt.

"What's the matter, Sarah?" Rachel demanded. "We're following all the rules!"

"Aye." Hope reached over and patted Sarah's arm. "You've naught to be afraid of."

"But what if we're caught?" Sarah said. "My papa will—"

"Then we simply tell the truth," Hope said.

Rachel pulled her mouth into a knot. "We won't be caught. We are experts at this now, are we not?"

Sarah squeezed her hands together like she was wringing out a rag. Josiah didn't understand much about girls, but he knew how Sarah felt. He was ready to start squeezing out his own hands.

Ezekiel went over to crouch behind Sarah on the other side of the fire. "Sarah," he said, his voice low and crafty, "what if you were walking home from Hope's house some gray winter afternoon when suddenly from out of the trees —Jonathon Putnam sprang into your path!"

Sarah gasped.

"Aye . . ." Ezekiel brought his lips closer to her ear. "And he reached out and snatched the basket of pies you were carrying home to the inn and flung them into the snow— and then—and then—he grabbed you by the arm, girl—" He curled his fingers around Sarah's wrist. She looked down at them, terror dancing in her eyes, "—and then he hurled you into the snow and then he—"

"No!" Sarah screamed.

She pulled her hands over her eyes, and Rachel gave Ezekiel a shove that knocked him backward onto the dirt floor.

"Stop it, Ezekiel!" Hope said.

"Idiot," Rachel said to him. "You've frightened the poor girl half to death."

"That's not half as frightened as she would be if that were really to happen," Ezekiel said, crawling back to his place beside Josiah.

"Well, he has that right at least," Hope said. "If we carry out our plan, Sarah, you won't have to worry yourself about such things."

"Aye," Sarah said in a wobbly voice. "Let's do it, then. But I can only help to plan it. I can't really do—"

"Good, then." Hope smoothed her hand over Sarah's skirt, and she was quiet.

"What about everyone else?" Rachel narrowed her eyes at Josiah and William.

"I know William is in," Ezekiel said. "Aren't you?"

It didn't surprise anyone that William nodded dutifully.

"What about you, Josiah?" Hope asked softly.

"Oh, he surely wants to!" Rachel cried. "I hate to admit it, but he is better than any of us when we actually get out there."

"Rachel, why must you talk about me as if I weren't even in the room?" Josiah said.

Rachel's eyes widened for a minute, and then she laughed. "My, my, Hope, your little brother is becoming quite the proper little soldier, eh?"

Josiah stood up in disgust.

"Where are you going?" Hope got up on her knees.

"I'm just not sure about all this," Josiah said. "Papa said he was to handle it, and I don't like not telling him, and—"

"You're afraid, aren't you, Josiah?" Ezekiel looked around at the rest of the Merry Band as if he had just made an amazing discovery. "He's afraid. For all his book learning and all the stories he has told us about friendships with Quakers and Indians and sailors—he hasn't any courage at all. Not when it comes to helping his own friends. His real friends."

"That's not true!" Josiah cried.

"Then prove it." Ezekiel looked around the circle again. "Let him prove it, then."

Rachel started to say something, but Hope put her hand out to stop her.

"I know you're just trying to be responsible, Josiah," Hope said.

Ezekiel snorted. "That's for sissies—and you're surely turning into one, Josiah. I never thought it would happen to you, but—"

"Shut it, Ezekiel!"

Josiah almost laughed. All three girls had shouted it at the same time.

"Come on, Josiah," Hope said. "We really need your help because you are the responsible one. You will keep us from making stupid mistakes." She looked at the others. "Right?"

Rachel and Ezekiel nodded in reluctant agreement. William and Sarah looked more enthused. Hope was begging him with her eyes.

"All right, then," Josiah said slowly. "But the plan has to be perfect. No chance of being caught or doing any damage—"

"All right, all right!" Ezekiel cried. "Let us get to it!"

As they tightened their circle around the fire to begin planning, Hope stole a glance at Josiah. *Thank you,* she said wordlessly.

Josiah sighed. Maybe it would be all right after all. Just this one more time.

✢ ⚜ ✢

Chapter Eight

It's so very odd, Josiah thought as he crunched across the hard-as-rock snow early the next morning. *Everything looks so different once you've decided.*

The Merry Band's plan had been completed by the last flickers of their little fire the day before, and everyone had made it home in time for dinner. With all of the pieces in place—Hope glowing with the confidence that things were about to happen and Papa still brooding over what he was to do—Josiah's doubts seemed to slip away.

Well, they hadn't exactly slipped away, he admitted to himself. He had just tucked them into a safe corner of his mind.

But this morning, while the moon still cast shimmery light on the hard snow and his boots crunched importantly on top of it, it seemed right. He had a job to do, and that was what mattered.

It was so early, not even the hardest-working of farmers was up. Only two black crows pecking at some leaves stuck to the snow looked at him, and they didn't seem to care what he did. They didn't even watch as he went down the snow-packed road and crept behind the trees that bordered the Meeting House. It was empty this early in the morning, but then, it always seemed empty to Josiah. He'd certainly never felt like God was there.

Being careful to keep low and stay behind the trees and thorn bushes, he left the Meeting House behind and finally came upon the parsonage. This was the only part of the plan that scared him a little. He was sure Ezekiel would be nervous, too, if he had ever met up with John Indian. He was more frightening than any real Indian Josiah had ever seen. Not knowing what the servant's routine was in the morning might make it a little hard to avoid him.

So, when he slipped up to the back of the woodshed, Josiah stayed on his knees and peered around in all directions. Slithering like a snake, he made his way to the shed door and examined the ground. Ah, he was safe.

It had snowed again last night, so yesterday's footprints would be buried. Now fresh footprints—deep, manly ones —led to the door and then away. John Indian had already gathered wood this morning. Josiah looked up. A faint trickle of smoke trailed listlessly from the chimney. As stingy as Reverend Parris was with warmth, John Indian wouldn't be coming back for more wood for a while.

Without making a sound, Josiah opened the door and

stepped inside. He gave his eyes a moment to get used to
the darkness and then he went straight to the spot where
the Hutchinsons' wood was sloppily piled. It was still there
—they hadn't even started to use it yet. Josiah shook his
head. It wasn't needing the wood that made them steal. It
was spite.

But there was no time to play with that thought now.
Josiah piled as much of the wood as he could carry into his
arms, leaving himself one free hand for managing the
door. Then, like a ghost, he eased himself outside and leaned
against the door to close it. Beside him, there was a gentle
thud.

Josiah sucked in air and grabbed at the wood to keep
from dropping it. As quickly as he dared he turned to look
—and all the air came out in one frosty puff. Nearby, a load
of snow that had been piled onto a birch branch had slid to
the ground. The snow was still flying up in a fine powder.

Sissy, Josiah said to himself, and he made his way to the
fence.

It wasn't easy carrying an armload of wood through
knee-high snow. But at least it was still fairly dark and the
fence was close by. In five or six giant steps, he was there.
His arms were glad to let the wood slide off and onto the
other side, where it nestled nicely under a big snow-laden
pine tree.

He took a second to look at it. That shouldn't be more
than Rachel could load onto her sled later today. And it
shouldn't be so much that John Indian or Tituba would
notice it was missing when they came out to get more

wood at dinnertime. Josiah snorted softly. It was sure Abigail wouldn't be coming out to carry wood. She probably wasn't even out of bed yet.

"You have to get up early in the morning to outsmart the Merry Band," he said softly to the dark windows of the parsonage. And then he slipped into the trees for home.

Joseph Putnam was quiet in school again that day, but Josiah only wondered about it in little flickers in his mind. In fact, he decided, it was a good thing. For their teacher didn't seem to notice that his three students were having trouble concentrating on their studies.

Although William, Ezekiel, and Josiah had their noses firmly in their readers and their fingers pinched around their quill pens, their glances bounced at each other like pebbles thrown against a rock wall. Josiah knew their every thought.

Has Rachel found a reason to run an errand to the Hutchinsons?

Did she find the spot where Josiah dumped the wood?

Was she able to load it all onto the sled and get it to the Hutchinsons' barn without being noticed?

It seemed like dinnertime would never come, and when Joseph Putnam finally opened the classroom door, Josiah was the first one to bolt through the doorway. His heart was hammering by the time he reached the Hutchinson kitchen, and he could barely catch his breath as he fairly fell through the door.

"There was no need to dash home, Josiah," Mama said

mildly. "We wouldn't eat all the dinner without you."

Although Josiah said, "Aye," he didn't really hear her. He had eyes only for Hope. Her back was to him as she stood at the fireplace spooning up venison stew.

Well, then, he wanted to shout, *did Rachel come? Did she leave the wood in the barn? Did you see it there?*

He was afraid the words would burst out on their own when she finally turned and greeted him with a smile that told the whole story.

"We'll be in need of wood before you return to school, Josiah," Mama said softly. "Let you get some now, and then get ready for dinner."

"Aye!" Josiah said.

His mother stared at him as he dove for the door and raced outside. He headed straight for the barn—and there it was, neatly stacked by the door. Josiah grinned as he scooped it into his arms and carried it toward the house.

"Fetching wood from the barn now?"

Josiah's grin faded, and he stopped in his snowy tracks. *If questioned, you cannot lie.* He had made that rule himself. He had to tell the truth.

Slowly, he turned to face his father. "Aye, sir."

His father's eyes looked into him, and Josiah's heart stopped beating. His father never looked into him like that without coming out knowing things. It would be useless to lie to those eyes anyway.

Papa opened his mouth again, but the sound of footsteps crunching across the snow stopped him. Hope was running breathlessly up to them without even a cloak.

"We have a visitor, Papa!" she said.

"Who?"

"Joseph Putnam. He says he's sorry to trouble you at dinnertime."

But Papa waved her off and strode toward the house. Josiah began to breathe again.

"Well, that was a stroke of good luck, eh?" Hope said. "Was he questioning you?"

"He was starting to."

"It's sure the barn is not a good spot. Perhaps Rachel should take the wood right to the woodshed, eh?"

"It's sure we shouldn't be doing this at all!" Josiah said. All the doubts he had tucked into that safe place in the back of his mind were clawing to the surface.

"Nonsense!" Hope took some of the wood from his arms and led him to the house. "Papa has far too much on his mind to worry about where you're fetching wood from. Didn't you see the look on his face when I told him Joseph Putnam was here?"

"Aye, but—"

"And that same look was on Joseph's face when he arrived. Something important is afoot, Josiah. We are doing naught but helping while Papa takes care of this ugly business, whatever it is."

They weren't to find out that day at dinner. In spite of the need to conserve on firewood, Papa had Josiah build a small fire in the fireplace in the best room, and he and Joseph Putnam ate their dinner there in private while Mama, Josiah, and Hope dined in the kitchen.

"Whatever they are talking about must be important," Hope said.

"And it's no business of ours. Hush now." Mama tried to look at them sternly, but her soft face melted into a smile. "Eat your dinner. We'll have some of that apple pie then, eh?"

Josiah dug into his trencher and tried to push the doubts back into their place.

The Merry Band had figured it would take only three days to move the stolen wood from the Parris's woodshed to the Hutchinsons'. Since everything was going so well, it looked as if that were going to happen. The only hitch was the problem of where to put the wood once Rachel got it to the Hutchinson farm.

Hope told Josiah to tell Ezekiel to tell Rachel to dump it behind the woodshed. Then it would look more like Josiah was bringing it from inside the shed than it did when he had to go to the barn to get it. It would be a little out of Rachel's way, but she'd manage.

But the next day, even though Josiah dumped the wood behind the Parris's fence without disturbing even a branch full of snow, Rachel did not appear at the Hutchinson farm. After dinner, Ezekiel met Josiah at the front door to Joseph Putnam's house and dragged him behind a pine tree.

"What happened?" Josiah whispered.

"Mama wouldn't allow Rachel to go on another errand to your house. She scolded her and said she was only try-ing to get out of her work to go and talk foolishness with

Hope." Ezekiel scowled. "This would be so much easier if Sarah would do her part. She should take a turn."

Josiah shook his head. If poor Sarah Proctor were caught by John Indian or even Tituba, she would certainly turn to stone right there on the spot.

The sound of a wooden whistle pierced the air, and both Ezekiel and Josiah fumbled for their whistle pouches. Ezekiel got off the first toot, and William joined them, red-faced and puffing.

"Joseph Putnam says we're to come in for lessons now —" He stopped and stared, wide-eyed, at both of them. "What's wrong? Was Rachel caught?"

"No, she didn't even go," Ezekiel said. "If your sister would—"

"She can't! She's too frightened—"

"You Proctors are a sorry bunch, then—"

"Are not!"

"Are so!"

"Stop!"

Josiah shot out his arms and caught both of them in their middles. Their voices cut off abruptly.

"Let us just decide what's to be done!" he said. "You sound like the Putnams, bickering so."

Ezekiel crossed his arms over his chest and sulked. "You decide, then," he said. "The Porters have done their part."

Josiah searched through his mind, throwing this idea aside and stepping completely over that one. He was about to suggest that maybe they'd gotten enough of the wood back anyway when William lifted his pale chin and said, "I shall fetch it on the way home, then."

Josiah stared at him. "How will you do that? You have no sled. I dumped more than you can carry."

"Then I shall have to make two trips."

Josiah had no answer for that. He could only stare harder. William was offering to do something really risky.

Someone else noticed it, too. Ezekiel cleared his throat loudly. "You shan't do it alone, then, William. If we go one at a time, we can each carry today's load, and it will be done. There won't be so much chance that we'll be discovered that way."

Josiah nodded. "All right, then. And I'll be lookout."

From above them, a window opened and Joseph Putnam stuck his head out into the biting cold. "Will you gentlemen be joining me today?" he shouted.

"Aye, sir!" they called.

As they ran to the house, Josiah thought to himself, *Joseph Putnam sounded better just then. Perhaps Papa and he have gotten rid of some of their doubts, too.*

✣ ⟡ ✣

Chapter Nine

Their capture of the firewood went so well that afternoon, Ezekiel wondered out loud if they shouldn't have planned it that way in the beginning. "Who needs those girls?"

Josiah looked over his shoulder. They were standing outside near the kitchen window, and he surely didn't want Hope to hear a comment like that. She was likely to come after Ezekiel with a butter press.

"Shall we do it that way again tomorrow, for our last load?" Ezekiel asked.

William shrugged.

"I suppose," Josiah said slowly.

Ezekiel's eyes danced. "Good, then. Tomorrow, Merry Band!"

The darkest hour is always the one just before dawn,

Papa had once told Josiah.

And Josiah was grateful for that on the last morning of the firewood plan as he made his way from the barn, where he had just fed the horses, cows, and chickens, and down the road to the parsonage. It was apparent that no one in Salem Village ventured out at this early hour, but he was still cautious. The darkness made a fine cloak.

He had just passed the back of the somber Meeting House and was slipping through the trees toward the parsonage, when out of the blackness, he heard something. It was different from the morning noises he'd heard the other two days, and he sank into a snowdrift to listen.

There it was again—a whistling sound, made by no bird he had ever heard in New England. It sounded like Ezekiel or William signaling to him, except it was softer. Could Ezekiel actually have decided to join him, just to be part of the "adventure"? Josiah scowled and listened some more.

Again a soft whistle, unmistakably from a wooden whistle. Josiah knew he couldn't blow his that softly, so he waited and watched. Slowly, he turned so he could make a circle with his gaze—and there she was, a tiny square of her blue shawl barely visible through the branches of the next tree. Josiah didn't bother to wonder how she had gotten so close without his knowing it. The Indians had ways he could never hope to learn.

In a moment, she was next to him.

"Wife of Wolf!" he whispered.

But she shook her head, and her face was stiff. Danger was close by, and there was no time for conversation. Josiah could tell that. He grew still and watched her.

Almost without seeming to move at all, she pointed toward the woodshed and put her fingers to her lips. He held his breath and waited.

Soon he heard the door to the woodshed slam shut. Then came the crunching of footsteps in the snow. John Indian appeared around the corner, right where Josiah would have been if the squaw hadn't kept him safely in the trees.

Something had obviously disturbed John Indian, because he stomped around the woodshed growling to himself. Finally, he went back inside and came out with an armload of wood that he carried to the house as if he planned to eventually throw it at someone. Only when he had disappeared inside the parsonage did Josiah breathe easily.

Wife of Wolf seemed to relax, too, and she smiled at Josiah.

"Once again, you saved me," Josiah said. "Thank you."

She nodded. The shawl had slipped from her head, and when she reached up to pull it around her ears again, the wooden whistle bounced on its leather strap against her chest. Without really thinking about what he was doing, Josiah grabbed it and curled his fingers around it.

"I gave this to my friend," he said. "His name was Oneko."

The squaw seemed to freeze.

"You must know something about him," Josiah said, "or else you wouldn't have this whistle."

The squaw shook her head, almost as if she were afraid. That was something Josiah had never seen in her before, but he pushed on. "Can you take me to him? Please? He was my friend. I miss him!"

Suddenly, the squaw stood up, and for a crazy moment, Josiah thought she was going to lead him to her Indian camp. Instead, she took him by the arm and crept silently toward the woodshed.

Josiah forgot about Oneko and clutched her hand. "No!" he said. "John In—the man knows the wood is gone— our wood. He went to tell Reverend Parris. They'll be back!"

Either the squaw didn't think so or she didn't care. She kept her hand firmly around Josiah's arm and went straight to the woodshed. He had no choice but to go with her, and once inside, he picked up half the remaining load as quickly as she did the other. Almost before he knew what was happening, they were back outside and headed for the fence.

Both dumped the wood to the other side, and Josiah stood with his jaw unlocked and his mouth hanging open. Wife of Wolf nimbly jumped the fence and began to gather the wood into her arms on the other side.

"Come!" she said in the low, grumbly voice Josiah had heard only a few times.

He obeyed and piled his own pieces of wood into his arms.

She looked at him as if waiting for instructions.

"My woodshed," he said. "But, Wife of Wolf, it isn't safe for you to be in the village."

She grunted. Her eyes said, *Foolish boy,* just as clearly as Hope's lips had ever said it. Josiah led the way. The sun had only just begun to rise when they dumped the wood inside the Hutchinsons' woodshed.

Josiah had to smile at her. "It's done! It's all done now."

She nodded, but she didn't smile. Josiah saw that she

was nervous. She was on a white man's property, where it wasn't safe.

"Josiah!"

His father's voice was like thunder cracking open the sleepy morning.

"Aye, sir!" Josiah answered automatically. He could see the fear flickering across the squaw's face.

"Where are you?"

Josiah snatched up an armload of wood and cracked open the door.

"Here, sir!"

"Oh. You're at it early this morning, then."

Trying not to open it any wider than the width of his own body, Josiah sidled out the door. It closed behind him as the squaw pushed it from the inside.

Papa came toward the woodshed, and Josiah hurried to him.

"You've become an early riser," Papa said. "It's a habit I like to see you develop. I've always thought God was much easier to find when the world was quiet. . ." His voice trailed off as his eyes came to rest on Josiah's load of wood. "Why is there snow on this wood?" he asked.

Josiah couldn't answer. He couldn't even look innocently at the snow in question and pretend he didn't know. He could only stand there and look into his father's eyes and hope his father didn't see anything in his.

"Will you answer me?" A storm brewed on his father's face.

If questioned, you cannot lie.

"Aye, sir, I will. Just this morning, the wood was—"

But Papa suddenly put up his hand. "Listen!" he commanded.

Josiah did. He heard a scratching sound from inside the woodshed. He looked wildly at his father.

"There is naught to panic over," Papa said. "'Tis only a mouse trying to keep warm." He turned on his heel and went toward the house. "See you chase him out of there later. Get you in to breakfast now."

As his boots squeaked across the snow, he left Josiah behind. It was all Josiah could do not to open the woodshed door and thank her—again. But he shifted the wood in his arms and followed his father toward the house. Later he would thank her. Now she needed a chance to get away.

But would there be a later? he wondered. She wasn't happy when he'd asked her to take him to Oneko. Maybe he had pushed too hard. With the firewood plan finally over, all the worrying and wondering about his Indian friend hurried to the front of his mind again. The thoughts were harder to think now, because he was sure he'd scared her away. He would probably never see Wife of Wolf again.

Ezekiel pouted the rest of the day when he found out his services weren't needed that afternoon. William just looked uneasily from Josiah to Ezekiel and back again.

He thinks he should be pouting because Ezekiel is pouting, Josiah thought. *He can't think for himself, and Ezekiel tries to think for everyone else. I'm tired of them both!*

But that made Josiah want to pout himself. Without

them, and with Joseph Putnam being so distant and there being no hope of ever seeing Oneko again, it was turning out to be a lonely winter.

Maybe that was why that night, when Hope made her suggestion, he didn't let the doubts stop him, even for a moment. Anything was better than feeling so alone.

It had actually started earlier that evening when Papa was reading by his rushlight, as always, and Mama and Hope were sewing. The knocker clattered on the front door, and Josiah was sent to answer. He returned to the kitchen with Ezekiel's father, Benjamin Porter. His eyes were alive the way Ezekiel's always were when he had news to tell.

"I've been to Ingersoll's Ordinary," he said. "You know how they gossip there."

"Aye." Papa rolled his eyes. "That's why I don't go there. That—and the fact that the Ingersolls are Putnam people."

"Aye, but it's a good way to get information, Joseph," Benjamin said, "and I have some I think will interest you."

Whether it interested Papa or not, it certainly interested Hope. Josiah watched her as she crept closer to Papa's chair so she could hear.

"There is talk, and I believe it to be true," Benjamin said, "that an entire load of firewood was stolen from Reverend Parris's woodpile."

"Of course he would say that." Papa's lips curled. "The man has gone mad over this firewood business."

"I think it may be true, though, Joseph," Benjamin said. "I heard it from his own servant, that John Indian he brought from Barbados." Benjamin chuckled softly. "He barely speaks English, but it wasn't difficult to tell what he was saying. He has a temper, that one!"

Josiah shuddered. Anyone who had never been tossed over the black man's shoulder didn't know the half of it.

Papa folded his big, rough hands under his chin. "So, has the good reverend accused anyone?"

Josiah held his breath, but Benjamin shook his head. "No. I think he's afeared, Joseph. He has so many people hating him now, he doesn't know which way to turn."

Josiah felt his father's eyes on him.

"Josiah," he said sharply.

"Aye, sir." Josiah lowered his eyes.

"Look at me," he said.

Josiah did. He was sure his father could read the words in his eyes: *If questioned, you cannot lie.*

But before his father could even ask the questions, Hope stood up and shrieked. Everyone whirled to look where she stood next to her father's chair. His rushlight had toppled onto the floor, and the tiny flame that allowed him to read in the dim room was racing across the rag rug under his chair.

"Joseph! Fire!" Mama cried.

Almost before the words were out of her mouth, Papa had torn off his vest and was on the flames, beating them furiously. The tiny fire was well out before Mama even got to it with her pan of water.

"Crack open a window. Let the smoke out." Papa's voice was shaky around its edges.

"Quick work, Joseph," Benjamin Porter said. "I have seen a small fire like that bring down an entire kitchen in the blink of an eye."

Everyone was quiet as Papa looked at Hope. "How did that happen?" he asked.

If you are questioned, you cannot lie.

"I believe I knocked it over, sir." Hope's voice was clear and strong. Josiah had to admire her for that. His own knees were shaking, and he had had nothing to do with it.

"You did?" Papa said.

"Aye. I believe so, sir."

Josiah held his breath, and he could tell everyone else was holding theirs as well. But Papa reached out and swallowed up Hope's shoulder with his hand. "See you be careful. A fire can be a hideous and horrible thing."

"Aye, sir," she said.

"Good, then. I shall take this burned rug outside, eh?"

"I'll come with you," Benjamin Porter said. "We have more to talk about."

"By the way," Papa said as they left the kitchen, "thank you for the news about Reverend Parris. Perhaps he is shaken up enough to see what is happening right under his nose in his very church. Nothing would make me happier than to see this village and its church reunited again."

Benjamin didn't answer. Josiah wasn't sure the Porters wanted to see peace at all. Like Ezekiel, they loved a battle.

Josiah was sure of one thing. What they had done had given Papa some hope. What could be bad about that?

Hope was thinking the same thing. He knew that when she wriggled into his cot beside him and began to whisper.

"It is time for another meeting of the Merry Band," she said. "Now, don't begin to lecture me about—"

"When shall we have it?" Josiah asked.

He could feel Hope staring at him in the darkness. "Well, right away. But aren't you going to—"

"I shall tell William and Ezekiel to tell their sisters. The day before the Sabbath, right before supper. In the old woodshed."

"Aye," Hope said softly. "You are truly brave, do you know it?"

Josiah smiled into the dark. He didn't answer, but inside he thought that perhaps . . . he was.

Chapter Ten

It wasn't until the next day that Josiah remembered something he wanted to ask Hope. Had she knocked Papa's lamp over on purpose to keep him from asking a question Josiah wouldn't be able to lie about?

If she had done it on purpose, that would mean she was willing to risk burning down their whole kitchen, perhaps their whole house.

If questioned, you cannot lie.

Josiah decided he wasn't sure he wanted to know the truth about that one. It might be better not to ask.

Besides, he had other things to think about. As soon as Ezekiel found out there would be another meeting of the Merry Band, he forgot to sulk, and William was, of course, immediately happier. And for some reason, Joseph Putnam was even beginning to act a little more like himself. On Friday, when the boys hurried out of the schoolroom, he asked Josiah to remain behind.

"I think I owe you a great apology, Captain," he said when William and Ezekiel were gone.

Josiah felt his eyes leap open. "You do, sir?"

"Aye. You and I have been friends for some time now. But of late I have been so wrapped up in my own thoughts and problems, I have slammed the door on you and left you standing outside my friendship." He put his hand on Josiah's shoulder. "I am sorry for that, Captain. Forgiven?"

Josiah knew his cheeks were turning pink as he shrugged. "Aye, sir. But you owe me nothing."

Joseph's eyebrows shot up. "Indeed I do! Friends owe each other a good deal—honesty for one thing. If you had a problem you thought I could help you with, I would be disappointed if you didn't come to me and share it."

Josiah pulled his own eyebrows together in confusion. "Should I have tried to help you with your problem?" he asked.

Joseph chuckled softly, but Josiah knew he wasn't laughing at him, the way so many grown-ups did.

"You probably could have helped me, Captain," Joseph said. "You are wise beyond your years. But as it turns out, I have solved my problem. At least I know what to do about it now, although it won't be easy." A shadow passed over his bright, fresh face, and Josiah watched it carefully. "That is part of what I wanted to speak to you about. When I do what it is I have to do, it may very well be that Ezekiel Porter will no longer be in our class."

Josiah's mouth fell open. "Why?"

Joseph Putnam folded his hands and rested his chin on the two pointer fingers he left sticking out. Josiah had seen him do it many times when he was thinking hard about what to say next.

"If it is agreeable to you, Captain, I would rather not say that yet. It may indeed be that Ezekiel will not be removed. Perhaps I am wrong about his grandfather. But it is always good to be prepared, and that is all I am trying to do for you. Now, I must ask you one favor."

"Aye," Josiah said.

"I would prefer that we keep this conversation between us. Please don't share it with anyone else, eh?"

"Aye," Josiah said again. "But if I am questioned, I cannot lie."

Joseph Putnam's face broke into one of his dazzling smiles. "Those are fine words, Captain. A good code to live by." He nodded thoughtfully. "I must remember that myself. And, no, if anyone asks you directly, don't lie. After all, I am not ashamed of the truth. I would simply prefer that it not be told just yet."

Josiah took his time walking home that afternoon. The sun was setting in a blaze, casting its pinkish-orange glow on the snow, and Josiah bathed in it as he strolled toward the farm.

Joseph Putnam's words were like a comforting hand coming down on his shoulder: *I am not ashamed of the truth. I would simply prefer that it not be told just yet.*

That was exactly what the Merry Band was doing. They weren't ashamed of having taken back the firewood that rightfully belonged to them. Nor were they ashamed of whatever it was they would have to do next to help their parents. If anyone asked, they would have to tell—unless a visitor interrupted them, or an Indian squaw made a noise inside the woodshed, or a lamp was knocked over.

But they would prefer not to say anything just yet. Other people might not understand. Just as Joseph Putnam was afraid old Israel Porter wouldn't understand whatever decision it was he had just made. It was something that might make the old man angry enough to yank his grandson out of Joseph's school.

And here I am thinking I am brave, Josiah thought.

"It is a providence!" Hope said as she, Josiah, Sarah, and William picked their way through the snowdrifts toward the old abandoned woodshed on Saturday afternoon.

"What is?" Sarah asked.

"That just when we needed you here so the Merry Band could meet, your father decided to bring you along when he came to talk over some business with Papa."

"Perhaps the adults are having their own Merry Band meeting," William said.

"I say it is a providence." Hope tucked her arm through Sarah's. "God must surely be with us."

I asked Him to be, Josiah thought. He had spent a lot of time looking for Him the night before as he lay in his cold cot in his cold room. It was hard to feel God nearby when your bones were rattling and your teeth were chattering, but Josiah had finally felt His closeness. He had asked Him if He would please bless the Merry Band and guide their footsteps.

He looked down at his leather boots, encrusted with ice and snow. They were on their way to the meeting place, and Sarah and William were miraculously with them. It must be what God wanted them to do.

Ezekiel already had a tiny fire going when they arrived, and his face was lit up brighter than its flames. "I know what it is we must do next!" he cried before Josiah even had a chance to sit down.

"Good, then," Hope said. "Let's hear it."

"We have naught to do but take down that fence Nathaniel Putnam put up on my father's property." Ezekiel crossed his arms over his chest as if the matter were already settled.

"I'm surprised your father hasn't done that already," Hope said.

"Aye, we are, too," Rachel said. "But I think our grand-father has some other plan in mind."

Josiah frowned. "If the adults have already decided what to do about the problem of the fence, perhaps we should stay out of it."

Ezekiel sighed noisily. "There you go again, Josiah. You are always so afraid to take a chance!"

"Josiah may be right, though . . . ," Hope started to say.

But Rachel put her hand on Hope's lap to stop her, and she herself leaned toward Josiah the way she would toward a small child. "Yes, you may be right, Josiah," she said. "Except I don't think what the adults have in mind has anything to do with taking down the fence."

"Then, I don't see what harm our doing it could do," Hope said slowly. "Does it follow the rules?"

"It won't hurt anyone," William said.

"Nor will it do any damage," Rachel said.

"We would be destroying a fence," Josiah said carefully.

"That's undoing damage," Ezekiel told him, his lip curled in disgust.

Josiah knew he wanted to add "Ninny" or "Stupid" to the sentence, and he felt his shoulders stiffening. Ezekiel could be so self-important sometimes, especially when he was putting someone else down.

"Of course, if we're caught or questioned...," Hope began.

"We cannot lie," they all said together.

We are not ashamed of the truth, Josiah added to himself. *We would simply prefer that it not be told just now.*

"Good, then," Hope said. "Now we need a plan, and I think Josiah should be in charge of it."

"Josiah!" Ezekiel came up on his knees and scowled so hard, Josiah thought his sharp cheekbones would pop through his skin. "It was my idea! I should be in charge of the plan!"

"If you are in charge, you're likely to get us all drowned in the Ipswich River or something!" Rachel said. "Shut it now, Ezekiel!"

"I won't!" Ezekiel shook his head like a wild man. "I want to be in charge!"

"And someday you shall be," Hope said. "But as long as you behave like you're doing now, like a baby boy, who of us is going to trust you to lead us?"

"I am not a baby! Josiah is months younger than I am!"

"Surprising, isn't it," said Rachel, "that he acts years older?"

There was a frozen silence. Everyone but Ezekiel looked admiringly at Josiah, and although his cheeks went strawberry red, the glow he felt in them was pleasure. But what really sent any lingering doubts skittering to the far corners of his mind was the look on Ezekiel's face.

His blue eyes seemed to sizzle with green, and they narrowed to a jealous point right at Josiah. He folded his arms, jammed them against his chest, and blew out a puff of air that sent his lips flapping in front of him.

Josiah turned his head to hide his smile. Good, then. If it would put Ezekiel in his place, he would be the leader.

So, with their little fire struggling to stay alight and their hands cramped and frozen around their quill pens, the Merry Band went to work. By supper time, they had a plan that they assured each other could not fail. Even Ezekiel was nodding in agreement, especially since Josiah had graciously given him an important job. The only piece missing was a time to carry out their plan. They had to do it at night, and getting out of their houses after dark was nearly impossible unless they sneaked out their windows. But Josiah had squashed that suggestion the minute Ezekiel made it.

"We must all keep our ears and eyes open for an opportunity," Hope said as they gave up thinking and put out the fire.

"I want to say something before we go," Sarah Proctor said suddenly.

They all looked at her in surprise.

"What is it, Sarah?" Hope said.

"I want to say that I'm sorry I couldn't take a job in this fence plan. I just—I simply get so frightened, I wouldn't be of any help. But I want you all to know that I believe in us and what we're doing."

Hope and Rachel both hugged her, while Josiah, William, and Ezekiel murmured thank-yous and got to the door as fast as they could before Sarah could slobber on them.

Why, Josiah wondered as they hurried home, did girls always have to gush so? It was one of the thousand things he didn't understand about them.

He did understand Sarah's feelings a little, though. It was hard to want to be part of something and not be able to because you were afraid and had doubts. Josiah smiled to himself. Well, he'd taken care of his doubts.

At least he was pretty sure he had.

✝ ✦ ✝

Chapter Eleven

*S*arah did find her chance to help—and sooner than anyone expected.

Monday morning, William came to school with his pale face looking as if it were about to explode with news. He darted his eyes toward Ezekiel and Josiah so many times during their first reading lesson that Joseph Putnam finally closed his book and twinkled his eyes at them.

"One thing I know for certain in this life," he said. "A person simply cannot learn a single new thing when his mind is already full to overflowing with something else. Suppose I go to the corner there and correct this arithmetic you did for me Friday, and you, William, empty your mind to Ezekiel and the Captain so that I can proceed to fill it up again. What say you to that?"

Three heads bobbed, and Joseph Putnam smiled. "I have thirty problems to correct. See you have your business taken care of by the time I have finished, eh?"

It is a providence, Josiah told himself as he scrambled to the opposite corner of the schoolroom with Ezekiel and William.

"What is it?" Ezekiel demanded first.

"I have a message from Sarah," William said.

Ezekiel pulled one corner of his mouth up. "Sarah?"

"Aye." William leaned in and lowered his voice as far as he could. "She was working in the inn yesterday when some folks came in between services at the Meeting House. She heard them talking, and they said that tomorrow night there is to be a meeting at Ingersoll's Ordinary to discuss the fact that Reverend Parris's salary is fourteen months overdue . . ."

William took a deep breath so he could continue, but Ezekiel cut him off. "So? What good does that do us? None of our fathers will go. They don't care about Reverend Parris's salary or anything else about him!"

"Aye, but they will!" William whispered. "Sarah heard them say that they are going to discuss what's to be done with those villagers who don't pay their taxes for the reverend's salary. And I myself heard Papa say that he would be there to protect his rights."

"I know my father won't go," Josiah said. "He vowed never to go into Ingersoll's Ordinary again after he and Mama were not voted into the church. He said so right in front of the Meeting House that very day!"

"But he is going!" William said, his pale eyes glowing. "That's why my father went to see your father on Saturday

—to convince him. And—" William crouched low so that the three of them were in a tight little knot in the corner, "—someone at our inn said that in his sermon yesterday, Reverend Parris mentioned *names* of people who were a threat to the society—and all three of our fathers were named, and your grandfather, Ezekiel."

"Ah." Ezekiel nodded with great wisdom. "And none of our fathers will allow their good names to be blackened without a fight."

William nodded too. "Aye. That's what Papa said. And there's more." His eyes danced. "Sarah has talked Mama into inviting all the goodwives to the inn for sewing while the men attend their meeting."

Ezekiel pulled his chin in. "That was *Sarah's* idea?"

"Aye," said William, "and proud of it she is. She even said if I didn't give you the message she would pull off one of my ears."

"Ouch," Ezekiel said.

Josiah was sure Ezekiel believed his own sister would do that, although Josiah couldn't imagine sweet, quiet Sarah laying a hand on her brother. However, a sister was a sister.

"So, if all of our fathers go to that meeting," Ezekiel was saying in a voice laced with excitement, "our mothers will go to the inn and we can get on with—our plan."

"How can we know that the men will all go?" Josiah asked.

They thought for a minute, and then Ezekiel looked over at their teacher, who had his handsome, oak-colored head bent over their arithmetic lessons. "There is one way to find out," he said.

Before Josiah could stop him, Ezekiel had crossed the room and was standing by Joseph Putnam's desk. Josiah was suddenly uneasy.

"Sir, may we ask you a question?" Ezekiel said.

Joseph looked up pleasantly. "Of course. What is it?"

Ezekiel crossed his arms like a courtroom lawyer. Josiah rolled his eyes at William.

"If there were to be a meeting that concerned taxes," Ezekiel said, "and perhaps your good name, would you attend?"

"Aye, I think so," Joseph said.

"Even if there would be men there who had no respect for you?"

"Aye."

"Even if it would be held at Ingersoll's Ordinary?"

"Aye, Ezekiel, I am going to the meeting," Joseph said quietly.

"Oh." The slyness went out of Ezekiel for a second, and then he hurried back to his friends.

"You see?" he said, as if he had just scored some rather large victory.

But Josiah didn't answer. He was watching Joseph Putnam. For as he turned to continue grading their work, his eyes were sad—*like he was just reminded of something,* Josiah thought.

When I do what it is I have to do, Joseph had said, it may very well be that Ezekiel Porter will no longer be in our class. Did that have anything to do with what was going to happen at the meeting tomorrow night?

But a tug at his sleeve from Ezekiel brought him back to what it was he had to do tomorrow night. And a clearing of the throat by Joseph Putnam brought them all scurrying back to their lessons.

"Ezekiel, suppose you read first," Joseph said.

He wants Ezekiel to learn all he can before he loses him, Josiah thought. *But why? Why would he lose him? The Proctors, the Hutchinsons, the Porters, and Joseph Putnam—they all think alike. They're like a grown-up Merry Band. What could change that? If Joseph Putnam broke from them, what would my father do? What would I do?*

"Will you be joining us, Captain?" Joseph asked softly.

Josiah nodded. Those thoughts would have to go into a corner with the doubts. They had a plan to carry out.

In fact, everything else except the fence plan was swept to that same corner of Josiah's mind. Even Oneko and the squaw weren't thought of as, over and over, Josiah went through the steps until he could see himself, William, and Ezekiel carrying them out. Hope, Sarah, and Rachel wouldn't be with them, of course. They would go to the inn with their mothers as part of the training to be goodwives themselves.

Only once did some tiny doubts spring up that what they were doing perhaps wasn't really right. It was Tuesday at noon when Josiah went home for dinner. At the table, Papa was unusually quiet as he bent over his codfish stew.

Suddenly, he set his spoon in his bowl and looked at Mama. "'Tis a fine stew, Deborah. It's well seasoned."

"Thank you," she murmured.

"But I cannot finish it now. I've a storm brewing within me, and I've a mind to go and pray it out."

"Aye, Joseph, of course," Goodwife Hutchinson said and added almost to herself, "May God be with you."

Papa stood up, but he stared at the table for a moment as if he might possibly find the answers he was looking for right there on the tabletop. He shook his head. "A man's soul cannot rest with a decision unless there is a peace in every scrap and tittle of it. I pray God gives me that peace."

He left the kitchen, stuffing his felt hat onto his head as he went. The other three Hutchinsons were quiet, waiting for his presence to leave with him.

"Papa is troubled," Hope said finally.

"Aye," Mama said. She sighed as if the trouble were all her own. "It's all this quarreling and bickering in the village. He wants peace for our people—and he's afeared this meeting tonight will only make things worse."

Hope slipped a glance at Josiah and said to her mother, "Is Papa going, then?"

Mama smiled softly as she stood up. "I think that depends on what God is telling him now. Come on, then, children, there is naught for you to worry over. Let's see to these dishes now, eh?"

While Mama and Hope cleared the table and turned its top for the afternoon's work, Josiah set about his job of filling his father's rushlight. As he pulled the rush leaves from the animal fat they were soaking in and placed them carefully in the lamp, he thought, *I wonder if Papa will be here reading by this lamp tonight or if he will go to the meeting.*

If Papa didn't go, William and Ezekiel would have to take down the fence by themselves. Perhaps that would be all right, after all. For after watching Joseph Putnam's sad eyes and seeing the uncertainty in his father's, Josiah's doubts tried to pry themselves loose from the corner where he'd stuck them. Would Papa be upset with them if he found out? If this was the right thing to do, why weren't they telling him? Were they lowering themselves to the same kinds of tricks the Putnams liked to pull?

The worst doubt of all was a new one. Both Joseph Putnam and Papa seemed very worried about something. It was always a great burden to live in this new country, Papa had said many times. But the deep lines in Papa's face and the sadness in Joseph's were for more than just the usual troubles. If the Merry Band carried out their plan and were caught, would that just add to the heavy load Papa already carried?

Josiah shook his head. The whole idea of the fence plan was to ease their parents' burden. Perhaps like Papa, he should go to God one more time and find a peace in every little part. He would have to do that.

But with the afternoon chores to do, and school after dinner, and supper-time jobs to take care of, there wasn't time.

Just before it snows in Massachusetts, hazy circles form around the sun. But there were no circles late Tuesday afternoon. The last of the sun was glittering on top of the snow that still covered the ground, crunchy in the cold.

"It's going to be a perfect night," Ezekiel whispered to him as they left Joseph Putnam's. "Remember, as soon as my father leaves for the meeting, I will meet you at the Merry Band's hideout."

"I know," Josiah said impatiently. Ezekiel seemed to forget that it was Josiah's idea in the first place.

"And see you bring William Proctor with you. He's a coward without one of us pushing him along, eh?"

Josiah grunted.

Ezekiel stopped and eyed him closely. "You aren't afraid, are you, Josiah? After all, they made you leader."

"No!" Josiah said. "I'm not afraid! I'm not afraid at all!"

To prove it, he picked up a handful of snow and balled it up to hurl at Ezekiel. Ezekiel shrieked with laughter and ran as the snowball flew in his direction. With it went all of Josiah's doubts.

The air was thick with tension at the dinner table. Papa poked at his baked apple as he brooded, and Hope and Josiah picked at theirs in nervous nibbles. Mama sighed as she cleared the trenchers away.

"My family ate like little birds tonight," she said. "You are still troubled, then, Joseph?"

Papa pushed himself back from the table. "Nay. The Lord is good. I have made a decision and I am able to stick to it now—come what may." He looked at Hope. "See you help your mother and then bundle up warm. I shall drive you to the Proctor Inn before I go to the meeting."

Josiah could hardly keep from collapsing with relief. He felt as if he had held his breath for three days.

"Josiah."

He jumped.

"You will be left to yourself. I trust you will be about your reading and your studies in our absence."

If questioned, you cannot lie.

"Perhaps Josiah should come with us," Hope said.

Josiah's head jerked up, but he saw the laughter in her black eyes.

Papa grunted. "Josiah has no need to learn to sew. Hurry along, then. I do not want these stiff-necked people to begin the meeting without I am there."

When he'd left the room, Hope gave Josiah a superior smile. *Where would you be without me, Josiah Hutchinson?* her eyes said.

Standing at the window, Josiah watched his parents head for the wagon in the dark. Hope came up behind him, wrapped in her cloak and hood, and tapped him on the shoulder.

"You'll need this tonight," she said. "It's fearfully cold out."

Josiah turned and she gave him a black woolen scarf.

"I remembered that you gave yours away to someone in Salem Town last summer," she said. "I was of a mind to make you another."

Josiah ducked his head as he took the scarf in his hand. "Well—thank—thank you," he said.

She grinned at him. "You still stutter when you're embarrassed. You're such an odd duck."

Josiah was afraid for a minute she would hug him. But instead she wrapped the scarf around his neck and whispered, "God be with you tonight."

This must be right, Josiah thought as Hope hurried across the snow toward the lantern Papa held up at the wagon. *Every scrap and tittle of it.*

Chapter Twelve

The Hutchinsons' wagon had barely disappeared around the bend in the road when Josiah heard William's whistle. He put one more small log on the fire in the kitchen to make sure it would keep burning while he was gone and hurried out to meet him. There was no time to waste if he would be back here with his nose in a book before the rest of his family returned.

Together he and William hurried through the darkness to the hideout. The night was cold and clear and crisp with snow as they ran.

"See you be careful of ice patches," William said. "I hit one and fell right on my backside on the way to your house!"

"All right, then," Josiah said. Normally, they would look for patches to slide on, but tonight it was all business. Ezekiel reminded them of that when they arrived at the old woodshed to find him already there, shivering in a corner. There would be no fire tonight.

"Where have you been?" he asked. "I've been waiting forever."

"You told me to wait for William," Josiah grumbled.

"And I couldn't leave until my father was well on his way," William said. "Besides, all the women are coming to my house, remember? Unlike you two, I had to sneak out."

Josiah hadn't thought of that, and he winced. John Proctor was a good, kind man but strict with his children. A doubt appeared like a filmy cobweb, but Josiah batted it away.

"Let's not bicker like the Putnams," he said. "We have work to do."

"Shhh!" Ezekiel said suddenly.

"I am the leader, Ezekiel," Josiah said. "Don't be telling me to shush!"

But Ezekiel waved him off and pinned his ear to the wall of the shed. Josiah and William did the same.

"What did you hear?" William whispered nervously.

"I thought I heard someone walking about," Ezekiel said. "But I don't hear anything now."

Josiah wanted to tease him for being a coward, but something in the air stopped him. Suddenly, everything was serious. This wasn't a game anymore, and he had to be a leader.

"It was probably just some snow falling off a tree branch," Josiah said. "That happened to me at the Parris's woodshed one day, and I thought it was John Indian coming."

Ezekiel straightened his shoulders. "That was probably it. Shall we go, then?"

Josiah cracked open the door. The night was perfectly still, so he waved to his friends to follow. Like three snow-bound chipmunks, they skittered away from the shed and into the darkness toward Benjamin Porter's farm. As they left the woodshed behind, Josiah stole one more look back at it. There was no one in sight. Their secret was still safe.

The village was strangely silent as they circled it. They stayed far from all the houses, but few lights winked in the windows anyway. Everyone, it seemed, was at the meeting or had gone to the Proctor Inn. The trickiest part would be slipping past Nathaniel Putnam's house, which was close to the Porter farm. Josiah scanned it carefully with his eyes as he passed it.

Suddenly, his heart skipped a beat. He saw a figure outlined in the kitchen window—a woman. *Of course,* Josiah thought. That had to be Marta, Nathaniel's wife. The Putnam women wouldn't go to Elizabeth Proctor's house. Marta must be sewing there in the kitchen while she waited for her husband to come home.

Josiah froze for a moment, and Ezekiel and William bumped into him from behind.

"What's the matter?" Ezekiel whispered hoarsely.

Instead of answering, Josiah pointed, and the boys gasped.

"Do you think she sees us?" William said.

Josiah watched her silhouette in the window carefully. Her head was bent over something in her lap, the way his mother's was when she was knitting or embroidering. She didn't look up or talk or anything, and slowly Josiah shook his head.

"She hasn't seen us," he said. "She's too busy."

"All right, then!" And Ezekiel started to charge on.

Josiah grabbed his arm. "We'll just have to be extra careful and hope the Putnam women are keeping an eye on their sons tonight."

When they reached Ezekiel's farm, he proudly showed them where he had buried the tools in the snow near the fence. The iron bar he handed Josiah was cold, and Josiah juggled it back and forth so it wouldn't freeze to his skin.

"Let's go to work, then," Josiah whispered. "William, you take that end and, Ezekiel, you work from the other. I'll carry the lumber and pile it over there."

They already knew all of that. They had been through it a hundred times, it seemed. It just made Josiah feel calmer to say it. William and Ezekiel nodded and went to work.

Fences in Massachusetts were built mostly to keep cattle in and to show neighbors where one's land ended and the other's began. They weren't meant to keep people out, and so they were put together loosely with a few wooden pegs. It didn't take long for the boys to pry the boards off and pile them on the other side of the line that Ezekiel's father had said truly divided his property from Nathaniel's.

"It *is* Nathaniel's wood," Hope had reminded them at their last meeting, "so when you take the fence apart, you should put it on his property."

"It's our wood if he's put it on our property!" Ezekiel had protested loudly.

Hope had looked straight at him and said, "If we don't return his wood to him, we're as bad as he is."

Josiah smiled to himself as he rocked a post back and forth to loosen it from the frozen ground. They weren't like the Putnams. This was a good thing they were doing. And they were doing it with deerlike speed. The job was going so well, in fact, that Josiah didn't feel like he had to remind William and Ezekiel of the escape plan. If something happened—if they heard someone coming or if one of them was caught—those who could were to run to the hideout. But it didn't look like there would be any need for that tonight.

Just then, from out of the lonesome stillness of the night, a wolf howled—a long, thin, soulful howl. Josiah leaned on the fence post for a minute and listened.

He hadn't heard the wolves since winter had started and the windows and shutters were closed so tightly at night. The howl was a friendly sound to Josiah, and he smiled to hear it. *My wolf friends are telling me all is well,* he thought. Saving the wolves was the first job of the Merry Band. Now maybe the wolves were watching out for them.

The thin post finally pulled loose from the ground and Josiah fell back with it into the snow. He giggled as he rolled over with his arms hugged around the wood.

"No playing around now, Josiah," Ezekiel hissed.

"Shhh!"

This time it was William who had shushed them. He

was returning from his last trip to the line to drop an armload of fence rails and he had stopped dead in his tracks,
eyes wide as two pewter plates.

"What is it?" Josiah asked.

"I heard a door slam!" William said.

Ezekiel snorted softly. "You didn't. You're such a rabbit,
William—you're hearing things. Come on. We've one more
post to pull and the job's done—"

He cut himself off as his ears picked up what both Josiah
and William had already heard. From the direction of
Nathaniel Putnam's house came the unmistakable sound
of boots crunching quickly across the snow.

Josiah felt William's eyes fasten on him in panic, and his
own thoughts spun as he looked around. A line of trees
separated them from the Putnam house. They could still
pull out the last post without being seen and have time to
run.

"Psst!" he hissed to William and motioned toward the
post with his head. Together they scrambled toward it and
yanked with two sets of arms until it came out of the ground.
William started to slide backward, but Josiah caught him
by the sleeve and hissed into his ear. "We have to run for
the hideout! Follow me!"

They would have to take a different route now, Josiah's
racing thoughts told him. If they ran straight toward the
hideout they would run right into whoever was after them.
If it was the Putnam boys—and who else could it be—
they would expect Josiah and his friends to run south to
Israel Porter's place. They would just plow through the

snow to the north, he decided. Then they would turn just above John Putnam's house and make their way back down to the hideout.

The footsteps and shouts were almost on them now, and Josiah turned with a jolt and ran. He heard William's heavy breathing close behind him as he leapt across an icy gully and began to run across the top of the frozen snow.

We're leaving them! We're going to get away!

That was his last thought before his boot caught on an icy patch and both feet shot out in front of him. All the air went out of him as he lay there on his back.

"Come on, Josiah! Get up!" Josiah could hear the tears in William's voice.

"I can't!" he said, gasping for breath. "Keep running! I'll catch up to you!"

But William took hold of Josiah's arm and with a wrench pulled him across the top of the snow and into a drift that had piled around the bottom of a huge spruce tree. As the footsteps pounded closer, William took an armful of snow and dumped it over the wide track he had made with Josiah's body. Then he dumped another armload over Josiah and some more on himself. They were buried in white except for their eyes as two pairs of clunky boots thundered by. They stopped a few yards away, and so did Josiah's heart. He squeezed his face to keep from moving or breathing.

"There are tracks here, but they stop!" Eleazer Putnam shouted.

"Shut it!" Jonathon hissed. "Do you want them to hear our every thought?"

It was quiet, and Josiah and William watched the feet shuffle around on the snow as the Putnams sniffed like hounds.

One of them must have motioned to the other because suddenly the tree Josiah and William were hiding under began to shake. They were climbing it! Clots of snow hurtled to the ground and the branches creaked and protested under their weight. Almost before they began, there was a loud thud and a groan. Josiah slid down further into the snow so they wouldn't see him—but not before he caught a glimpse of Jonathon flat on his back in the snow.

Jonathon gargled for air and then sat up. "They aren't here," he grumbled to Eleazer. "We're going back to the house."

"But what about—"

"Shut it!" Jonathon growled. "I have no time to waste on those brainless boys anyway. I want to be the first to tell my father what they've done to his fence."

"But how do we know it was them? We didn't catch them—"

"Shut it!"

Josiah waited until their voices had faded away into the night before he dug himself out of the snow and peered through the lower branches.

"They're gone," he whispered to William.

William poked his head out, and Josiah covered his mouth to keep from laughing out loud.

"What's wrong?" William demanded.

"You're a living snowman!" Josiah said.

William made a face and flung a handful of snow at him. Josiah scooped some up, and then he let it drop.

"Where's Ezekiel?" He grabbed at William's snowy sleeve. "You don't think they have him, do you? We have to go back for him!"

He started to stand up, but William yanked him down. "He ran," he said.

"When?"

"As soon as we heard them coming, he ran."

Josiah nodded and blew on his hands, which were frozen into icy claws. "He's gone to the hideout, then. He remembered the escape plan."

William scowled at the snow. "He could have stayed and helped us."

Josiah stared at him in surprise. "Do you think he ran out on us, William?"

William shrugged. "Let's go," was all he said.

"Aye." Josiah brushed the biggest clumps of snow off his clothes. "He'll be worried about us."

William grunted.

Although the Putnam cousins had long since reached their house, Josiah tried to keep even his breathing quiet as he and William made their way toward the hideout. It was hard, though, for the frigid night air singed his lungs as he ran, and the icy patches were like huge, hard puddles everywhere they turned. Josiah pulled the black scarf Hope had made for him up over his nose and dug his chin into his chest. If he kept his head down, the cold didn't bite so hard at his face. That helped as they slipped and slid across Wolf Pits Meadow.

That was also why he didn't see the flames until they were nearly on top of them and William clawed at his arm. "Our hideout!" he cried. "It's on fire!"

Josiah shook him off and tore across the icy ground toward the blaze.

"Josiah, no!" William screamed behind him.

But Josiah didn't stop. "Come on!" he screamed back over his shoulder. "Ezekiel is in there!"

Chapter Thirteen

Even in the harsh chill of the night, the fire burned hot on Josiah's face as he careened across the ice toward the burning shed. He reached down and filled his arms with snow.

"Ezekiel!" he screamed as he hurled the snow clumsily at the fire. "Ezekiel, are you in there?"

He had to get to the door. He had to pull it open and get Ezekiel out of there. The blaze roared in his ears as he slushed through the snow that had already melted around the flaming hideout—but still he screamed. Maybe Ezekiel had fallen asleep. Maybe the smoke had choked him. Maybe the door was stuck and he couldn't get out—

"Ezekiel!" he cried once more. But his lungs filled with fiery air and he doubled over to cough. Blinded by the smoke and choking on its gray curls, he tried to gather up some more snow. A pair of arms grabbed him from behind and pulled him away.

"No!" he screamed at whoever it was. He tried to shake loose but the arms were firm, and they pushed him down to the ground. He sputtered for air, and hot tears burned in his eyes. He tried to scream for Ezekiel again, but something blue and wet came over his face. He struggled to breathe—and then he was gone.

It was quiet when Josiah woke up. Very quiet—and very cold. Where was he? Why was he sleeping outside in the snow?

With a jerk he sat up. The fire. The woodshed. Ezekiel!

Wildly, Josiah looked around. He was lying several yards from the hideout, now a pile of charred wood with only a few tendrils of smoke still rising from it. Beside him, William was crying quietly. But there was no Ezekiel.

"William!" Josiah tried to say. But his throat cracked and only a scratching sound came out.

"Josiah!" William cried. "You're alive!"

"What happened? Who put the fire out? Where's Ezekiel?"

Josiah was standing by now, and William scrambled up and grabbed at Josiah's jacket.

"The fire went out by itself. I guess the snow kept it from going any farther." William wiped his sleeve across his eyes. "But I never saw Ezekiel. I don't think he was in there."

"Of course he was in there!" Josiah was crying, too, and the tears hurt his throat. "Where else would he have gone?"

"That woman looked around in there when the fire was

out," William said. "I don't think she found any—any—bodies."

Josiah's head turned sharply. "What woman?"

"I don't know," William said. "I never saw her before—"

"What did she look like?"

"I couldn't see her—but—Josiah—" William's red-rimmed eyes widened, "I think she was an—Indian!"

The image of something blue coming down over his face splashed into Josiah's mind. Something blue and wet that had blocked out the smoke and let him breathe again.

"I don't know where she went," William said. "She just dragged you over here and then she put that stone in your hand and just—disappeared."

Josiah slowly opened his hand and looked down at a flat, smooth stone that had been curled up in his fingers.

"What is it?" William asked.

But Josiah only shook his head. He didn't know why the squaw had given him a rock. What good was a rock now, anyway? Ezekiel was dead. He had to be. When you burned, there was probably nothing left of your body—just like there was nothing left of the woodshed.

Josiah shook with a sob. *Ezekiel's dead and it's my fault! I was supposed to be the leader. I was responsible. I thought I was some kind of warrior—and I wouldn't let him be the leader . . .*

His thoughts were choked off by the sound of voices coming from the direction of Thomas Putnam's house. Josiah and William looked at each other in horror.

"That's Thomas Putnam's voice!" William whispered.

"The men are back. Let's go, Josiah!" He grabbed Josiah's whistle pouch, stuffed the rock inside, and gave him a shove toward home.

"But—Ezekiel . . . ," Josiah sobbed.

"He isn't there, Josiah. Come on!"

"Good heavens!" someone shouted from afar. "There's been a fire!"

William tugged at Josiah's jacket and pulled him loose from his spot. Still sobbing, they whipped through the trees and left the remains of their hideout behind.

Even as he bungled across the snow and up to the back of his house, Josiah could see the wagon coming up the road. The light of the lantern shone through the poke holes in the shape of an H, and Josiah knew it was his family. He flung open the back door and slammed through the storage room and into the kitchen. He stopped dead and looked around. How strange. Everything here was peaceful. The last of the fire flickered in the fireplace. His books lay open on the table as if he'd been reading and had stepped to the cupboard for a slice of bread. A sob escaped from Josiah's chest as he looked at his quiet home. How could it all look the same when everything had changed? He was responsible for someone's death. And if questioned—he had to tell the truth.

Josiah thought of all the ways he had answered his own questions. He'd gone ahead with the plan because he didn't want Ezekiel to think he was afraid. Because he wanted to make proud Ezekiel Porter jealous. Because Hope had puffed him up, telling him he was the leader, the best, the smartest. Because he wanted to help his father and Joseph Putnam, even though Papa had told him not to.

None of those reasons made any sense now, even to him. Surely they wouldn't to Papa—not in a hundred million years—because there wasn't peace in every part of his decision.

Josiah ran to the window and watched as Hope jumped from the wagon into Papa's arms. As soon as her feet touched the snow, she craned her neck to peer toward the house. But Josiah didn't signal. *If questioned, you cannot lie . . .*

He lunged for the door to the hallway and took the steps of the spiral staircase two at a time as he ripped off his cold, soaked clothes. He had barely flung them under his cot and burrowed under his quilts when he heard the front door open. If questioned, you cannot lie. But if you are asleep, you cannot be questioned.

Although he pretended to be deep in slumber when Hope came into their room and stood over him, whispering his name, Josiah did little real sleeping that night. Every time he dozed off, he jerked awake with the picture of Ezekiel coming toward him with his blackened arms stretched out. Finally, toward dawn Josiah began to cry, and he had just cried himself to sleep when Papa knocked on the door and called him for chores.

So it was with swollen eyes that Josiah entered the schoolroom that day. He was late, but only William was there before him with Joseph. Josiah's heart fell to the toes of his boots as he sank heavily into his chair. Ezekiel wasn't here—because Ezekiel was dead.

Joseph Putnam didn't know about it yet, Josiah decided, for he didn't say anything, but merely started the lessons right away. In fact, Joseph didn't say much of anything, and Josiah noticed that the old sadness seemed to be back in his teacher's eyes.

The morning dragged on, and little was learned in the schoolroom that day. Josiah was tired and frightened and could see nothing on the pages of his books but the charred remains of their hideout. Joseph gave them their work and retreated to his desk, where he sat with his head down. William looked nervously at them.

By dinnertime, Josiah thought he would explode if he didn't get out of the classroom, but when he finally burst outside, he couldn't go home either. He didn't want Hope to ask him questions. He'd managed to avoid her this morning by not even going into the kitchen to eat break-fast. He wasn't hungry now either. He only wanted to sit somewhere and decide what to do next.

He found a place on Joseph's rock wall, toward the bottom of the hill where his big house sat. He perched on the wall in the sun and pulled his knees up to his chin. But the minute he rested his head on them, he started to cry again.

As soon as the town found out about Ezekiel—as soon as old Israel Porter started making noises with all his influence—they would surely know it was Josiah who had caused it. He'd be placed in the stocks. Thrown in prison in Salem Town. Hanged, even.

But that wasn't what made Josiah sob into the knees of his breeches. They could punish him all they wanted, but none of it could hurt as much as the thoughts that screamed at him in his own head. If he had been responsible. If he had listened to his own doubts. If he had insisted, like his father said, that there be a peace inside him with no ripples—if he were the leader they had all expected him to be—Ezekiel would be here still.

I would give anything to have him standing here telling me it was my fault the hideout burned down, Josiah thought as he sobbed. *I would give anything. What must God think of me now? I can never go back to Him . . .*

"Josiah," a soft voice said behind him. "What's wrong, son?"

Josiah made an attempt to smear his sleeve across his eyes as Joseph Putnam's fine, shiny boots came over the wall.

"You'll need to do more than that to hide that many tears," Joseph said, sitting beside him. "Something must be terribly wrong, Captain. What is it?"

Josiah shivered with one last sob. If anyone in the world would understand—would be able to help him—that would be Joseph Putnam. But even with the kind young man waiting patiently beside him, Josiah couldn't find the words.

"Ezekiel's dead!" he finally blurted out. "And it's my fault! It's all my fault!"

"Ezekiel—dead?" Joseph said.

"Aye. He burned in the fire—"

"What fire?"

"I didn't start it, but if I had been a better leader—or if I had never agreed to the plan in the first place—it wouldn't have happened! He would still be alive!"

"He is still alive, Captain."

Josiah blinked through his tears at Joseph.

"At least he was early this morning when he came to my house in his father's snowshoes to bring back my books."

Josiah shook his head.

"It's true," Joseph said. "I told you once his grandfather found out about a decision I made, he would probably take Ezekiel out of my school. And that is exactly what has happened."

All Josiah's thoughts seemed to fall into a heap inside his mind. He could only stare at Joseph.

"He was here—this morning? You *saw* him?"

"Aye. He was as cold and hard as his grandfather stalking into my hallway, but yes, he was alive."

Josiah could see then the signs of the storm raging inside Joseph Putnam. Although his eyes drooped sadly at the corners, his mouth was set in a hard line, one Josiah didn't see there often.

"I—I'm sorry you lost Ezekiel," Josiah said.

"As am I, but thank you, Captain. He is a smart, impetuous boy, and he needs schooling if he is to turn all of that energy in the right direction. We can only pray that his grandfather will find it for him elsewhere, eh?"

"But you're the best teacher in all the world!" Josiah cried.

Joseph's sad eyes twinkled. "And you've met many teachers, have you, Captain, in your travels?"

Josiah's cheeks burned and his eyes swam as he fumbled around for words.

Joseph reached over and patted his knee. "Have you a handkerchief in that pouch of yours? I think your nose could use some attention."

Josiah had never carried a handkerchief in his whistle pouch in his life, but he opened it anyway. The only thing there was a wooden whistle—and a smooth, flat rock. Josiah stared at it. It was just a stone, probably from the bottom of the river. But as he turned it over, his eye caught something painted on the other side.

"What's there?" Joseph asked.

Josiah held it out for him to see. "I'm not sure," he said. "But I think it's a picture of a wolf."

Chapter Fourteen

"**M**ay I?" Joseph asked.

Josiah nodded, and Joseph picked up the stone tenderly and cradled it in his hand. His eyes shone over it—like it was a kitten he held, Josiah thought.

"May I ask where you got this?" Joseph said. "You don't have to tell me, but I'm interested."

Josiah sucked in a frosty puff of air. No one else in the world knew about the Indian woman. Not even William, really. Although he had seen her, he didn't know that Wife of Wolf and Josiah were friends. *If questioned, you cannot lie*—and right now, Josiah needed Joseph Putnam's trust.

"An Indian woman gave it to me," he said. "A friend of mine."

He held his breath as Joseph continued to look at the stone. Then Joseph brought his eyes up to meet Josiah's.

"You've not gone home to dinner, and you must be hungry," Joseph said. "Would you like to share some hot cider and bread with me?"

Josiah nodded in surprise. Joseph tucked the rock back into Josiah's hand and led the way toward the house.

Although Josiah had been to Joseph's great house many times other than for school, he had never been in his teacher's study, and that was where he took him now. Josiah looked around with wondering eyes as Joseph stoked the fire in the tiny, handsome stone fireplace.

It may have been the most beautiful room Josiah had seen in his eleven years. The walls were lined with oak that had been rubbed and polished until it shone in the firelight. The window that overlooked the hill beyond was of genuine glass, and its panes were large and square so that little got in the way of the sparkling view of the snow and trees.

There was a desk in the room and two bright blue chairs with cushions that invited Josiah to sink into one of them. But he remained standing and looked at his reflection in the shine of the small round table that stood between the chairs.

"Come in, Constance," Joseph said softly in the voice he reserved for his pretty young wife.

When Constance Putnam came in, carrying a tray with two steaming mugs of cider and a round, brown loaf of bread, Josiah ducked his head and murmured, "G'day." She was by far the prettiest girl in Salem Village or Town, and her very presence always tied Josiah's tongue into knots.

She was Ezekiel's cousin, and she had the same wide Porter eyes, but her cheekbones were rounded and pink.

Josiah's thoughts veered off. *Ezekiel.*

If Ezekiel had gone to the woodshed last night when they'd heard the Putnams coming, he would have known it was burning, and surely he would have waited there for them or come back to help. And if he hadn't gone to the woodshed, where had he gone?

Josiah shook his head. He didn't want to think the only answer there could be. Ezekiel had done nothing other than run home—to his own house—leaving William and Josiah only two steps ahead of the Putnams.

"Won't you sit down, Captain?" Joseph said.

Constance was gone, the door was closed, and the fire slowly warmed the room. Josiah shoved thoughts of Ezekiel aside and plumped into one of the soft blue chairs.

Joseph motioned for him to take a cup of cider while he rummaged through the volumes on a bookshelf and pulled out a notebook with gold-edged pages.

"Your Indian friend has given you a fine gift, Captain." He sat opposite Josiah and placed the notebook on the table. "And it is not one to be taken lightly."

"Isn't it merely a rock with a drawing on it?" Josiah asked.

"You don't know the Indians well yet, do you?" Joseph said.

"No," Josiah admitted.

"You will, I have a feeling," Joseph said. "They seem to want you to know—and that is, of course, the only way you can find out their special secrets—if they want you to know."

"Do you know about them?" Josiah asked.

Joseph nodded. "Somewhat. God has allowed me that privilege, as He is obviously allowing you."

"God?" Josiah said. "But—Reverend Parris says the Indians are heathens!"

"They aren't covenanted Christians, surely. But does that mean we cannot learn something from them about the world God has made for us?" Joseph Putnam took the notebook gently into his hands and looked across the table at Josiah. "Would you like to know what that gift means that you've received from your friend?"

Josiah felt his eyes spring open. "Aye!"

Then he watched as Joseph slowly opened the book—as if he were being careful not to disturb any of the secrets hidden inside. He turned several pages, lifting each one with his fingers and letting it fall softly against the others until he found the page he was looking for. Slowly, he turned the book around, and Josiah gasped.

Sketched there on the page with a finely tipped pen was a drawing that exactly matched the one on the rock. To make sure, Josiah pulled it from the whistle pouch and stared—first at it, then at the notebook.

"Ah, that is the one," Joseph said, almost in a whisper. "The Wolf. Teacher. Pathfinder."

"How do you know that?" Josiah asked. "Where did this book come from?"

Joseph chuckled. "The book is of my own making. I

made the drawings from the gifts I received—and from those I saw on the rock walls."

Josiah's questions stopped, and he just stared.

"If you promise to drink some of this cider and eat enough bread to keep a bird alive, I shall tell you." Joseph's eyes twinkled. "But I don't want to have to tell Deborah Hutchinson her son starved at my hands, eh?"

Obediently, Josiah took a bite from the warm bread, but he didn't taste a crumb. His eyes were fastened on Joseph as he began to talk.

"Just a few years ago, when the better part of my schooling was done and I was waiting for God to tell me what He would have me do next, I had a mind to go out into the wilderness to search for my path. Something like what Jesus did—though I surely do not compare myself to Him."

Joseph stopped for a minute, almost as if he were checking to be sure he hadn't offended God, Josiah thought.

Leaning back in his chair, Joseph continued. "I felt close to God out there in nature, but it is a dangerous country, this Massachusetts, especially if you don't know the ways of its two kinds of natives—the animals and the Indians. I had one meeting with a bear that sent me running straight into an Indian village. I was somewhat—well, in truth, I was terrified. But the Indians are not always the warlike people so many have made them out to be. Like any human being, they will attack if they feel they have been wronged. But the point here is that the Indians became my friends. I shared my faith with them—I told them of our Lord and the promises He made to us and as I got to know the Indians, I began to understand where some of their beliefs have come from. They know much about God's world."

It was quiet in the room as Josiah collected his thoughts.

"How did you learn all this," he said finally, "when they don't speak English?"

"I learned some of their language, they learned some of mine. People can communicate with each other if they are willing to bend, and if they do not, it will never happen. That is why there are many in this very village who cannot understand each other, even when they speak the same language."

A dark shadow passed over Joseph's face, but he brushed it away with a wave of his hand and smiled at Josiah. "I am sure you have had conversations with your Indian friend."

"Aye," Josiah said. "With both of them."

Joseph's eyebrows went up, but he didn't ask questions. He smiled and said, "In my conversations with my Indian 'family,' I learned that this wolf you have in your hand is the symbol for the teacher, the pathfinder. If the Indian woman gave you such a gift, it is because she sees that in you. The rock is supposed to remind you about that something you have to do."

Josiah opened his palm again to stare at the stone, and for a moment he thought he felt it burning his palm. Carefully, he set it on the table.

"What's the matter?" Joseph asked.

Josiah frowned. "Isn't it a sin—I mean, to use false— false things in your life to . . ."

His voice trailed off and he looked helplessly at Joseph.

Joseph made pistol fingers and rested his chin on them as he looked at his student.

"Are you worshiping that stone, Josiah?" he asked.

"No, sir!"

"Are you using it to make some decision that God could better help you with?"

"No."

"This is not witchcraft, Captain," Joseph said. "I see it as a sign that someone cares about you. Someone wants you to think about the path you will take from here. Someone wants you to be free from the battle you're carrying on inside yourself. I think that is what God wants for you, too."

Josiah smiled shyly. "God has never given me a rock."

Joseph nodded toward the stone. "Perhaps He has—through one of His other children. Your Indian friend. In any case, God has given you other gifts."

"Aye," Josiah said slowly, but he wasn't sure exactly what those gifts were.

"Do you recall a story I read to you from the Bible last summer?" Joseph said. "About your namesake?"

"Josiah! Aye, I do!"

"Good, then. And what was Josiah's job—according to God, that is?"

Josiah didn't even have to work hard to remember, for he'd thought of the story many times since he'd first heard it.

"Josiah's duty was to remind his people of what God's teachings were because a lot of them seemed to have forgotten."

"Aye, and that's a gift—that story." Joseph warmed his

hands on his mug as he looked thoughtfully into the cider. "It seems to me that God is trying very hard to tell you something. It could be that your job is to be a teacher, to remind your friends of what their duties are to God—to keep them on the right path."

"It was," Josiah said sadly. "But I failed. My responsibility is over, and I'm not going to be the leader anymore."

Once again Joseph's eyebrows shot up, and this time he didn't smile. "I don't think you have much of a choice, Captain. If the ship is sinking, do you jump overboard and say, 'I give up! I've failed!'?"

Josiah couldn't look at him. He stared down at his hands, which were clenching the pewter mug in his lap. Suddenly, he felt Joseph's fingers under his chin, pulling his face up to meet his gaze.

"If you have made mistakes, then face them, Captain. God is with you. He will never let you fall, as long as you are honest." Joseph's face softened. "What was it a friend of mine told me not long ago? If you are questioned, you cannot lie. Eh?"

Slowly, Josiah nodded. "Aye."

It was snowing again when Josiah walked home late that afternoon at suppertime. The windows in the Hutchinson kitchen were already coated with white when he got there so that even the firelight from inside didn't flicker on the panes and welcome him home. With no candles dancing for him, and no faces in the window smiling at him, the house seemed so empty—just the way he felt inside.

But it wasn't empty. He knew that the minute he pulled open the heavy front door and heard the angry voices shouting in the kitchen. One of them was Papa's.

The other two belonged to Thomas and Nathaniel Putnam.

osiah tried to close the front door without a sound, but the minute its latch caught, there was an abrupt silence in the kitchen.

"Josiah, is that you?" Papa called.

"Aye, sir." Josiah dragged himself to the door and peeked into the kitchen—at a rather frightening scene.

Mama and Hope were crowded near the fireplace with their backs turned, trying to ignore the shouting all around them. Nathaniel and Thomas Putnam stood at one end of the table, leaning across it toward Josiah's father, who leaned from the other end with eyes blazing. Papa's face was pale and lined. Those of the Putnams were as red as Josiah had ever seen them.

But it was the air that scared Josiah. It sizzled with anger, the kind of anger that often exploded into punching and screaming. This was no ordinary argument between the Putnams and the Hutchinsons where Papa would quietly ask them to leave. If anyone were leaving, they were sure to be thrown from a window as far as Josiah could see.

"Come here, Josiah." His father didn't take his eyes off his unwelcome visitors.

Josiah closed the door behind him and approached his father as slowly as he dared. He needed time to think. Why were they here? Would they accuse him? Did they know?

Frantically, his eyes went to Hope, but her back was turned, and even the cautious glance she darted at him over her shoulder gave him no answers.

Josiah took a deep breath. It didn't matter anyway. There was only one thing he could do. Joseph had said it. The Indian woman had said it in her way. Maybe God was saying it. He had to be honest. He had to be the responsible one.

"Ach! There's the wretched boy!" Nathaniel reached out to grab Josiah's arm as he crossed the kitchen. But before Josiah even felt his fingers on his sleeve, his father was on him, wrenching him out of the way.

"Do not touch my son," Papa said in a low voice. "I shall ask the questions, and if any punishment is to be meted out, I shall be the one to do it. Is that clear, Putnam?"

Nathaniel's face turned purple, and he sputtered on the table. Thomas took his arm. "See that you do it, then, Mr. Hutchinson," he said. "We have wasted too much time here already."

Joseph Hutchinson gave them both a hard look before he turned Josiah to face him. His hands weren't rough, but they were firm.

"Nathaniel claims a fence he recently built was torn down last night while the villagers were at their meeting at Ingersoll's Ordinary. Benjamin Porter claims it was his property and Nathaniel had no right to build on it, so I would assume it was Benjamin who tore the fence down, or one of his sons or nephews. But—"

"But I have already been to their homes, boy!" Nathaniel blasted at Josiah. "And it was none of them! Giles Porter was at the meeting with his grandfather. And that other— what is his name . . ."

"Ezekiel," Thomas said, as if the name tasted bad in his mouth.

". . . his father says he came running to him as he left Ingersoll's to tell him that there were prowlers on the edge of the property. It was my property he was talkin' about— he thinks it's his father's—"

Thomas put a hand on his stammering brother's arm and said not much more calmly, "The point is that as much as Benjamin Porter hates all of us Putnams, he isn't responsible for taking down my brother's fence, nor his son neither. But someone is, and we have reason to believe it was you, boy!"

Thomas thrust an accusing finger at Josiah, and Nathaniel backed it up with a furious nod. But Josiah wasn't frightened. He'd grown cold as he listened to them and his eyes went to Hope. She had the same look of utter disbelief on her face that Josiah knew was on his.

Not only had Ezekiel run off and left him and William to face the Putnams alone, but he had told his father that there were "prowlers" on his property. He hadn't just abandoned them. He had turned on them.

That was all Josiah could think. His father's voice brought him back to the room.

"If I may speak now," Papa said pointedly, *"in my own home."*

Thomas and Nathaniel pulled themselves back and began to brush imaginary dirt from their vests. Papa turned to Josiah.

"Thomas Putnam says he has reason to believe you were involved because John Indian caught you before in the Parris's woodshed—"

"He is capable of committing a crime was all I was saying," Thomas Putnam cried. So much for letting Papa speak in his own home. "He even planted his sled there to make it look as if the wood had been stolen from *him*—"

But Papa continued as if Thomas had not interrupted him. "You were later seen taking firewood early one morning from Reverend Parris's woodshed. That is as far as his accusations had gotten before you came in, so I need now to ask—" He shifted his piercing gaze to the Putnams. "Who is it that made this observance?"

"Why, Reverend Parris's niece, Abigail Williams," Thomas said.

Josiah could feel Hope stiffening on the other side of the room.

"And why did she not come forward with this information before, when the subject of Reverend Parris's supposedly stolen firewood first came up?"

Nathaniel could contain himself no longer. His knotted red fist came down on the table with a bang. "That is not the point, Hutchinson!" he screamed—so loudly that the flame in the lamp shuddered. "The point is that your son is a troublesome, vicious boy who has caused my own son no end of trouble—"

"Your son?" Papa said.

"Aye!"

"Jonathon Putnam? Boy of some fourteen years? Taller than my son by two heads?"

"The same, yes!"

"The same Jonathon Putnam you have bragged about in every public place in this village. Strong as any ox. Needs no education—has the intelligence of a Boston judge. This same Jonathon has been caused 'no end of trouble' by my Josiah?" Papa looked down at Josiah, elaborately pretending to see him for the first time. "I would certainly match Josiah's wits against your son's in an instant, Mr. Putnam, but for physical strength, Jonathon has him by virtue of age alone—"

"Hutchinson, you are deliberately straying from the subject at hand!"

Papa sobered and stared hard at Nathaniel. "What is the subject, Mr. Putnam? Just what is it you have come to say?"

Thomas cleared his throat. "He has come to say that—"

"I want to hear it from him!" Papa said.

Nathaniel looked at Papa and then past him. With his eyes fastened to the wall, he spurted out his words. "It has

been decided among the Putnam clan that I will not hold
the boy responsible for his actions in this. He is naught
but a child and a foolish one at that. But I do hold you
responsible, Mr. Hutchinson. I am filing a suit in Salem
Town court tomorrow against you for the destruction of
my property. If you cannot keep your boy in hand, then
you must pay the price."

There was silence in the kitchen, and Nathaniel looked
pleased with himself. He stepped behind his brother and
nodded until Josiah thought his head would bounce to the
floor. Josiah looked fearfully at his father, waiting for his
reply, but it seemed there was more.

"Now, then." Thomas Putnam tucked his thumbs into
his waistcoat. "There is another part of this that has not
yet been mentioned, but I am man enough to tell you now
so that you be not surprised in court when—"

"Get on with it!" Papa gritted his teeth. Josiah knew his
temper wouldn't hold much longer.

"Last night, an outbuilding of mine was also burned to
the ground."

Josiah felt Papa lock up like a dead bolt beside him. "You
had a fire?" Papa said, his voice genuinely shocked. "I've
not heard of this! Was anyone injured—your animals—
your goods?"

"Nay," Thomas said, almost as if he were disappointed.
"The building was—not being used. But it was purposely
burned—at the same time the fence was being torn down,
I'll warrant you."

"Ah, Josiah," Papa said tightly, without looking at him.

"These men have the utmost respect for you. They think you can be in two places at one time!"

"I think nothing of the sort, Hutchinson!" Thomas cried. "You continue to put words in my mouth! What I think is that the boy was not working alone. I think he had—accomplices!"

Josiah wasn't sure what an accomplice was. He only knew he wanted these men out of his kitchen before the truth could become any more twisted. When his father started asking him questions—and he would ask, he knew that—it would be hard to untangle all of this.

"Thomas," Papa said, "we have already established that you think my son is responsible for every ill that befalls your miserable family. Tell me what you intend to do about it and be on your way."

"With pleasure," Thomas said, with a gleam of delight in his eyes. "I, too, am going to file suit against you. We shall all meet in court in Salem Town some two weeks hence, eh? You and Nathaniel and I. Would it had happened long ago, Mr. Hutchinson. Once the court rules in our favor, perhaps we can all let this ridiculous quarreling be done with—"

"That will never happen," Papa said evenly, "as long as people like you refuse to let bygones be bygones. This suit of yours will solve nothing. Now, out of my house."

"Are you saying you will refuse to appear in court, Mr. Hutchinson?" Thomas said almost gleefully. Josiah expected him to begin rubbing his hands together at any moment.

"I am saying, out of my house."

Josiah hunched slowly down into his collar, and he saw Hope and his mother doing the same. If the Putnams didn't leave the kitchen before Papa had to say it again, they had no one to blame but themselves for what would happen.

"Will you be there?" Thomas insisted.

"OUT—OF—MY—HOUSE! NOW!"

Even as he backed out the door, away from Joseph Hutchinson's towering and angry form, Thomas shouted, "You will receive a summons, Hutchinson! You dare not blink it!"

Nathaniel, on the other hand, scurried from the room like a terrified mouse.

It took a few minutes after they were gone for the air to change. Papa stood with his back to his family, one big arm propped on the doorjamb and his head bent as he pulled his temper back to the place where he kept it hidden.

Mama hurried to the table with a bowl of porridge, and Hope followed with trenchers and spoons. But when Papa turned around, it was clear he had no interest in food. He was only interested in Josiah.

"Sit you down," he said. His voice was quiet. Too quiet.

But Josiah sat without trembling. There was nothing to do now but tell the truth. God is with you, Joseph had said. Josiah was glad. He would need Him now.

Papa impatiently pushed the trencher of porridge out of the way and sat beside him. From under his hooded, sandy brows, he looked into Josiah.

"Did you indeed steal firewood from Reverend Parris's woodshed?"

"No, sir, I did not steal it. I only took back what was ours—what was taken from me when I tried to deliver it."

"Even though I told you not to put yourself into the affair?"

"Aye, sir."

"Do you respect me, Josiah?"

That one surprised Josiah, and he swallowed hard. "Yes, sir!"

"Yet still you disobeyed me. Why?"

Right now Josiah had no idea. Hope and the others had made it seem so clear, clear enough for him to agree to it. But at this moment, with his father looking into him, yearning for answers, he didn't have a clue.

If questioned, you cannot lie.

"I do not know, sir," he said. "But I meant no harm. I only meant to help."

"And the fence?"

"Aye. I took it down."

Papa's eyebrows sprang up nearly to the top of his forehead, and Josiah could see he was truly surprised. That only made him feel worse. That kind of disobedience wasn't something Papa expected of him. He expected better from him.

"Why?" Papa asked.

"To help end the war."

"What war?"

Josiah swallowed hard. "The cold, bitter war you talked

about last fall—between the villagers—that keeps us all from worshiping together . . ."

His voice trailed off as he watched something strange cross his father's face. It was nothing hard, nothing like anger. It was more like understanding, as if Papa had suddenly started to put the pieces together in his mind.

He coughed and went on. "And this fire Thomas Putnam talked of—did you start that, too?"

"No, sir!"

"Do you know who did?"

"No, sir!"

"Did you know of it before tonight?"

Josiah nodded. "Aye, I did. I—I was there and I saw it burning. I tried to put it out, but it burned to the ground by itself."

Papa ran a hand through his hair. "What were you doing all the way on Thomas Putnam's property when moments before you were at Benjamin Porter's taking down a fence? Why did you go there?"

Josiah took his time answering. He had to be careful here—and even at that, he slipped a little. "We—I—I was chased away from the Porters' by some boys, and I ran there to escape."

"Who were they?" Papa asked.

Josiah hesitated. Up until now, it was only himself he was condemning. He hated mentioning anyone else's name because he was responsible. He had to be the responsible one now. Even if it was the Putnams—couldn't someone else find that out?

"Who was it, Josiah?" Papa said. "Your very silence tells me you know. Who was it?"

"Jonathon and Eleazer Putnam," Josiah said quietly.

"You're certain of this?"

"Aye, I saw them from where—I—was hiding."

Josiah put emphasis on the "I." He'd almost bungled it before and said "we." And that was one thing he was sure of. If William's and Ezekiel's parts in this—or even the girls', for that matter—were discovered, it would have to be because they confessed themselves. He had been the leader. He would take the blame.

Ezekiel wouldn't do that for you, a small, ugly voice whispered in his ear.

But Josiah shook it off. Ezekiel didn't have a wolf stone in his pouch and the respect of people like Papa, Joseph, and the Indian woman to win back.

Papa stayed quiet as Josiah thought. When Josiah looked up, his father put his hand on his arm. "Everything you have told me is the truth, then," he said.

"Aye, sir."

For a moment, Josiah's eyes flickered over Hope. She sat across from him at the table, toying with her spoon and not daring to look at him. He was glad she hadn't tried to make excuses so he wouldn't have to answer the questions. He felt as if a bag of stones had been removed from his shoulder. But it did surprise him that she didn't speak up. Didn't admit to her part in the plans. Didn't stand behind him.

It surprised him—and for the first time in his life, he

was disappointed in his sister.

Papa pushed his chair back and stood up. "Good, then. If I receive a summons, indeed I shall go to Salem Town and settle this matter. I see no problem, particularly if Benjamin Porter can prove that the fence was on his property." He stopped and smiled an unhappy smile. "Unless he decides to sue me then."

"Benjamin Porter would never do that, Joseph," Mama said. It was the first time she had spoken, and Josiah looked at her quickly. She had tears in her eyes.

"Ach! I don't know what to think anymore," Papa said. "I believe in our side of things. It's the methods I'm not sure of. Joseph Putnam is sure, and that has cost him dearly."

Josiah's ears perked up, but Papa fell silent and then shook his head as if to clear it. "As for you, Josiah, what's to be done about this matter of your disobedience?"

All eyes were on Josiah—except Hope's. She kept hers firmly on her bowl of porridge.

"I—I—" Josiah stopped and swallowed hard. "I don't think you should have to take responsibility for my actions, Papa. I am responsible. I should take the punishment, not you."

Papa's blue eyes widened. "Do you mean—go to court? Stand trial?"

Josiah nodded. "Aye."

Across the table, Hope's head came up, and her dark eyes looked at him in horror. Slowly, she began to shake her head.

"Joseph, please—no!" Mama cried. "He's but a boy!"

"But I am not a foolish boy, as Thomas Putnam said!" Josiah bit his lip and tried not to shout. It was bad enough to disagree with his parents. It was twice as bad to shout at them. "I am responsible. I want to go to court, Papa."

Tears began to splash down his mother's face.

"God will be with me, Mama," he said to her. "When you do what's right, He doesn't desert you."

The words came out clear and strong, but still Josiah wished someone would hurry and tell him they were true.

"Good, then," Papa said softly. His big hand came down on Josiah's shoulder and squeezed it gently. "We shall go to court together and you can answer your own questions, just as you have done here. I will be a proper lawyer for you, eh?"

It was only then that the tears began to form in Josiah's eyes, and he looked up at his father through a shimmer.

The eyes that met his were filmy, too, with a look of pride.

✛ ⁕ ✛

$\mathfrak{I}$t was quiet for a long time in their room that night —for so long that Josiah thought Hope had gone to sleep. He had almost drifted off himself when her bed curtains parted a crack, and she said, "Why didn't you tell on us?"

Josiah didn't move. "Why didn't you tell on yourself— and help me?"

"If questioned, you cannot lie," she said. "But I wasn't questioned."

Josiah laughed out loud.

"Shhh! You'll bring Papa in here!" she hissed.

But Josiah chortled on until she sprang from her bed and slid into his, plastering her hand over his mouth until he was quiet.

"What is so funny?" she said.

"That rule was about being honest, Hope," he said.

"So?"

"Do you think it's honest just because you don't lie?"

"What do you mean?"

"There's also telling the truth even when you're not asked to."

"What good would it do for me to tell on myself?"

Hope propped herself up on her elbow, letting the cold air in under Josiah's quilts. Angrily, he snapped them from her and turned his back.

"What good would it do?" she said again, leaning over him. "I was part of the plan, but telling that wouldn't help you in court—and why did you say you wanted to go to court yourself anyway, Josiah? That was—stupid! You'd only have been whipped or something if you'd just kept your mouth—"

It was Josiah's turn to clamp his hand over her mouth, which he did as he thrashed from under the covers and sat up to face her.

"Don't ever call me stupid again," he said, his face close to hers. "I am not stupid. I am doing what I know is right, and none of you are going to talk me out of it this time. And if you are smart, you'll do what you know deep in your heart is right, too, Hope Hutchinson."

There was a surprised silence before she peeled his hand away. "And what is that?" she asked.

"What does God tell you?"

She crossed her arms over her chest and tilted her chin. "That if we are to hold the Merry Band together, we cannot give away its activities unless we are asked directly. I am staying quiet so we can continue our work. We'll just have to be more careful next time."

He looked at her closely through the darkness. "Do you really believe that?"

"Aye, I do."

"Then you'll have to carry on without me. I won't be part of it anymore."

"Don't be st—" She stopped and tugged on her thick tangle of black curls. "I know Ezekiel betrayed you—all of us. He isn't welcome in the Merry Band. But you—there's so much to be done."

"You heard what Papa said. It was disobeying him, and I won't do that anymore. Now, please leave me alone so I can sleep."

She grabbed the sleeve of his nightshirt. "Not until you tell me it's all right that I didn't jump in and come to your aid tonight."

"No."

"Josiah, you are doing what you think is right. I'm doing what I think is right. What is the difference?"

Josiah turned over again and shut her out with his back. "The difference is that I don't really think you believe it's right. I think you're just afraid."

"Afraid!"

He didn't answer. With a flounce, she yanked back his covers and thudded angrily to her own bed. Josiah heard the curtains snap shut, and he felt the old hatred settle over the room.

God, he prayed silently, *doing what's right is good—but*

no one told me it would be this lonely.

It stopped snowing before morning, and there were playful piles of snow in the windows and long icicles hanging before them—the kind Josiah, Ezekiel, and William liked to use for swords.

But none of it looked like much fun to Josiah as he trudged to Joseph Putnam's for school. He didn't feel like playing, and especially not with them.

He was glad that Ezekiel wasn't coming to school anymore. But William was another thing. Why hadn't he confessed? It didn't occur to Josiah until he saw his friend running happily across the snow up to Joseph's house that maybe William didn't know they'd been found out. Surely when he did, he would stand beside Josiah. After all, he had saved Josiah from the Putnams. He'd shown bravery that night, covering them both with snow as they hid . . .

Quickly, Josiah went for his whistle, taking a moment to hold the wolf stone in his hand before he blew his signal. William stopped and looked around cautiously. Josiah tooted again, but William turned and hurried toward the front door.

Josiah leapt from behind the tree. "William!" he called.

William couldn't ignore him this time, and slowly he swiveled to look at Josiah.

"Didn't you hear my whistle?" Josiah asked as he slipped and slid toward him on the snow.

"I guess so," William said.

He looked at the toe of his boot, and Josiah felt an

uneasiness growing in his stomach.

"They've discovered the fence, the Putnams have—and they've accused me."

William's eyes flickered with fear.

"I told my father the truth," Josiah said. "The Putnams are taking him to court over it, but I'm going, too."

William's pale blue eyes bulged from their sockets. "To court? To stand trial, Josiah?"

"Aye. I have to."

"No you don't!" William's voice trembled. "Your father can do it for you! The court puts people in *jail,* Josiah."

That thought hadn't occurred to Josiah, and it didn't mean much to him now. He looked hard at William. "I didn't tell him or anyone that you were with me."

William's face broke into a trembling smile, and Josiah even thought he saw tears in his eyes. "Thank you!" he said. "My father— he would whip me sure if he knew I was part of it."

Josiah felt his face crinkling as he fought to understand what William was saying. "Didn't you know that before we started?" he asked.

"I never thought we'd be caught—and we weren't."

"Well . . ."

"I saw to that, Josiah. I saved you and me from being caught red-handed. They can't prove that you did it. No one saw you—"

"Unless Ezekiel tells," Josiah said.

William's face wilted. "Ezekiel? Why would he—"

"Do you know where he went when he left us that night?"

"I know he went home and left us there, but—"

"He went to find his father at Ingersoll's Ordinary and he told him there were prowlers on the property."

Slowly, William's mouth fell open, and for a long minute Josiah watched him struggle.

"I would never do that to you, Josiah," he said finally.

"He did it to all of us!"

William shook his head. "Not all of us. Just you. You're the one who's going to court."

Everything grew still around them as Josiah stared at his friend. Then without any warning, even to himself, he put out his hand and shoved William into the snow.

"I thought you would do the right thing and stand behind me," he said over his shoulder as he stalked away.

"If they ask me, I won't lie!" William called out to him. "I promise!"

But Josiah couldn't answer. There were too many lonely tears clogging his throat.

During a New England winter, it is hard to remember that spring will ever come again. As far as Josiah was concerned, there would never again be green and pink buds on those naked trees. There would never be peepers to catch in those frozen ponds. There would never be grass to roll in under all that snow or brooks to wade in under all that ice or even a warm sun to turn his face up to above those gray clouds.

That was just as well, he decided as he ambled home from school through the bitter cold a few days later. He had no one to do any of those things with anymore, anyway. Oneko was probably gone forever. William, Ezekiel, even Hope, had shoved him out into the cold and left him there by himself. He felt as lonely and brittle as the skinny little branches that shivered and trembled in the sharp chill of the afternoon. It couldn't get much worse.

And then it did.

He had just rounded the bend in the road at the base of Thorndike Hill when a voice called out, "Hello, boy!"

He looked up to see Abigail Williams hanging on the fence in front of her uncle's house. She was bundled up in a dark blue cloak and hood, and only her taunting face peeked out.

He didn't say anything but tried to hurry past her.

"You are a rude boy, Josiah Hutchinson," she said.

"Aye," he mumbled.

"Well, at least you admit it. Will you be that honest when you go to *court?*"

Something stopped Josiah's boots in the snow, and he turned to look at her. A crooked smile played on her face.

"Aye, I am going to be honest," he said.

She leaned toward him over the top rung of the snow-covered fence. "You're going to tell them everything, then?"

"Aye."

"That you took firewood from us and tore down Nathaniel Putnam's fence and burned down Thomas Putnam's shed—"

"I didn't burn down that shed." Josiah tried to keep his voice calm, but the mean glint in Abigail's eyes made it hard.

"Who did, then?" she asked.

"Perhaps you should tell me."

"I?" She tossed her head back and laughed until her hood fell to her shoulders.

She has hair the color of a mouse, Josiah thought. *She's not nearly as pretty as Hope, for all she acts like she is. She's nothing but a small, mean, wretched girl, and I don't know why I'm wasting my time with her.*

He turned to go, but she stopped him with her next sentence.

"I do know who burned down the shed," she said. "But the court never will. And do you know what they'll do to you for destroying other people's property, Josiah?"

"No," he said, "and I don't care."

She threw her leg over the fence and jumped down to stand beside him. Her narrow green eyes bored into his like nails. "Oh, you'll care enough when they tell you they're going to put you in *jail,*" she said.

Josiah just stared at her as she continued.

"Do you know anything about the jail in Salem Town? Because I do. My uncle goes there to pray with the prisoners. He comes home and tells horrible stories about it to Betty and me—to keep us from breaking the law and ending up there."

She had his attention now, and she knew it. Josiah stood as still as one of the fence posts as she leaned back against the rails and crossed her arms.

"A cell in the Salem Town jail is only big enough for one person to stand up in. You can never lie down. You can barely sit. And of course, if you do, you'll be sitting with the rats and the beetles and the remains of the rotted apples and eggs that they throw to you once a day for your meal." She slanted a grin. "When it's summer, you boil in the wretched, hot stench of the place. And when it's winter— well, Uncle says he has gone to visit prisoners who have frozen to death standing straight up in their cells and no one even noticed."

Josiah backed away, shaking his head.

"Oh, yes, Josiah," she said, nodding. "My uncle wouldn't lie to me. It's a wretched place, and you are very likely to end up there."

"You're a horrid girl," he said.

Her thin lips blew out in a laugh. "If I'm the horrid one, why is it you that's going to jail?"

"I'm not going to jail!" he cried.

She laughed again in her hard, cackling way. "We'll see about that, boy!"

Josiah took off running. He wanted to get as far away from her as he could, as fast as he could.

But her harsh laughter rasped in his ears long after he'd left her behind. And no matter how hard he tried to shake them loose, her words stayed in his head.

"Josiah."

He turned at the barn to see his father standing there with one of the horses.

"What are you running from? What's after you, boy?"

Rats! he wanted to cry. *And beetles and stinking cells that freeze you to death!* Instead, he shook his head.

"Nothing, sir."

"I received our summons today," Papa said.

Josiah felt his throat closing and he couldn't answer.

"We're to appear in court on Monday next. I've a mind to leave on Saturday so that you and I can attend meeting together on Sunday. We'll stay with Phillip English. I'm off to Israel Porter's now to see if we can borrow his sleigh for the journey."

"Porter?" Josiah's heart rose. Perhaps Ezekiel had confessed, too, and was going to Salem Town to stand by his friend. "Will the Porters be going with us, then?"

Papa looked puzzled. "No, son. Why should they?"

Josiah's heart sank again, and he shrugged. "No reason," he said. *No reason at all,* he thought as he slowly walked away.

Chapter Seventeen

Jail.

The smell of it. The sound of it. The sight of it.

That was all Josiah could think about. When he tried to read in school, the shadows of iron bars covered the page. When he closed his eyes to sleep at night, he imagined himself curled into a frightened ball on a dirt floor. When he dreamed, it was of skeletons hanging their bones through the bars in one last plea for forgiveness before they died.

He would awaken drenched with sweat in spite of the frosty air that hung over his cot. There was a time, not long ago, when he would have crawled into Hope's big curtained bed and told her every detail while he stopped shaking. She'd have told him sleepily to go back to his own bed, but then she would have thrown an arm across his back and hummed until he drifted off to more peaceful dreams.

That was out of the question now. He couldn't talk to Hope anymore for fear he'd blurt out something in front of his parents—something like, "Why are you letting me do this all by myself? Why don't you take your share of the blame?"

And she couldn't even seem to look at him. She slipped past him with her eyes down whenever he came into the room—*almost as if she's ashamed,* Josiah thought. *Almost as if she's afraid.*

But thinking about fear always brought him back to thoughts of prison cells with rotting food, and he did everything he could to avoid those thoughts. He even took the long way home from school every day so he wouldn't have to go past the parsonage and risk running into Abigail.

But by Friday, even trying to hide from the frightening thoughts wasn't working. He was nearly crawling home at dinnertime just south of icy Peter's Meadow, his head crowded with pushing, shoving fears, when a thin whistle halted his dragging steps.

His heart jumped. Was that William whistling to him? Or Ezekiel?

When he saw the blue shawl emerge from the brown underbrush, he was almost disappointed. But the smile that crumpled Wife of Wolf's face into a hundred happy lines coaxed a smile out of him, too. At least he had one loyal friend left in the world.

"Hello." He reached into his whistle pouch and pulled out the stone. "Thank you," he said as he held it out.

She smiled and nodded. Then she placed her own hand

over Josiah's palm. When she pulled it away, another stone lay next to the wolf.

He looked at it closely. Painted in the center of the smooth snow-white stone was a black bird. Its beak was bent low, just the way the crows curled theirs against the cold.

"Is it a crow?" Josiah asked.

But, of course, she was gone.

Josiah slipped twice on icy patches as he tore back to Joseph Putnam's house, and he was covered with snow by the time he pounded on the front door. Joseph answered with a napkin in his hand and his mouth full.

"What's happened, Captain?" he said in a voice muffled by venison stew. "Have you run into a blizzard, then?"

Josiah stuck out his hand and opened his fingers. "I've received another gift!"

Joseph's eyes stopped laughing and he stepped back. "Come in, then. Let's see what this is about, eh?"

Josiah stomped the snow off his boots and peeled off his jacket in the hallway as he hurried after Joseph toward the study. His teacher had the gold-edged notebook off the shelf before Josiah could get the door closed.

"It looks like a crow to me." Joseph stared at the stone again.

"Aye, I'm sure of it. I see them all the time in the snow, and they curl their beaks under, just like that!"

"You're an observant young man," Joseph said as he gently turned the pages. "That is what makes you such a fine student of life. Ah—the crow."

They were standing in the light of the window, and Josiah went up on his toes to study the drawing Joseph Putnam had made. It was almost an exact match for the painted version on Josiah's stone. Even the finely drawn feathers were the same.

"That's it," Joseph said with a satisfied smile.

"What does it mean?" Josiah asked.

Joseph's clear eyes looked at him. "It is the Indian sign for law," he said quietly.

Josiah felt his heart skip a beat. "Law?"

"Aye."

"But Joseph, how does Wife of Wolf know that I'm going to court?"

"I don't think she does. But I think she knows from your troubled look that your spirit is troubled also. You're in need of the perfect laws of God to guide you."

Josiah looked at him blankly.

"Suppose we sit down and I will read to you what I gathered about the crow from the Indians," Joseph said.

So, once again Josiah perched on the edge of the blue chair and craned his neck to see while Joseph read his fine handwriting on the page below the picture.

"The Indians believe the crow is the keeper of all sacred law. But human law is not the same as sacred law. If a human obeys the perfect laws as given by God, he has naught to be afraid of." Joseph looked up at Josiah. "Your Indian friend wants you to clearly see right and wrong and have a powerful voice to speak out for it, especially when what the world sees as right and wrong seems out of balance to you."

Both of them were quiet as Josiah continued to stare at the crow in his hand.

"I've written here," Joseph went on, "that as we learn to follow the guide of sacred law, our sense of being alone will vanish."

Josiah felt his face slowly break into a smile. Joseph Putnam put a gentle hand on his arm.

"I want you to remember something, Captain," he said. "The principles I have just read to you, about God's law being perfect, are Christian principles. That stone you hold in your hand won't help you in the courtroom. It isn't some magical charm."

"Does the Indian woman think it is?"

"I don't think so. I think it's merely a reminder. The real strength comes from God."

Josiah nodded softly. "Aye. I see." And perhaps for the first time, he truly did.

"Now, then." Joseph returned the notebook to its shelf. "What say you to some venison stew? I dare say Constance is tired of eating by herself, eh?"

Although Josiah's cheeks immediately began to turn pink, he followed Joseph happily into the dining room. Suddenly, the world looked somewhat less lonely. He didn't want anybody to have to sit alone.

On Saturday morning, Hope was already out of bed when Josiah woke up. It wasn't a restful night, and he opened his eyes groggily. He'd fallen asleep praying, and he had dreamed of being in court with a judge who had a face like a crow. There were chores to be done, though, before he left for Salem Town with Papa, and wearily he swung his legs out of bed.

But when he reached the barn, the cow had already been milked, and the chickens fed, and the horse watered. When he went to the woodshed for firewood, Hope greeted him at the door, a pile of wood already in her arms.

He stood in the doorway, gaping at her.

"If you're going to stand there staring, I shall probably drop all of this on your foot," she said.

Josiah stepped aside and watched as she stumbled toward the house under her heavy load.

"Was it you who did my chores for me?" he asked.

"Aye."

Something in her voice made Josiah hurry after her. When he looked at her face, he saw she was crying.

"Don't look at me," she said.

"Why?"

"Because I'm miserable!"

Josiah took half the load of wood and walked beside her toward the house.

"Is it because I'm going to court?"

"Yes! Why do you have to do this, Josiah? Why can't you let Papa do it, and then we could just go on and everything would be the same as always—"

"No it wouldn't!" Josiah cried. "Not inside of us. We would always know Papa took our punishment."

They had reached the kitchen door, and Hope stood in

front of it, crying softly. "I thought what we were doing was right—I truly did. Why does it all seem wrong now?"

"Because we were following our own rules instead of God's," he said.

She looked at him out of red-rimmed, puffy eyes that were streaming tears.

Mama poked her head out the door just then. "Where is that firewood, my dears?" she called. "Come on, then. There's breakfast to be cooked."

"You can ask Joseph Putnam the rest," Josiah said. "Just go to him and ask him about the crow."

"The crow?" she said as Josiah pulled open the door and went inside the house. "Josiah—the crow? What are you talking about?"

But Josiah had no time to explain, for there was breakfast to eat and a small bag to pack. When he was ready to climb into Israel's borrowed sleigh, Hope ran to him across the snowy yard and pressed a package into his hands.

"Corn cakes, with blueberries—your favorite," she said.

Tears filled her eyes again and she turned away.

Come with me, Josiah wanted to say. *Come with me and we'll do what's right together. Perhaps we can share a cell in the jail,* he added.

With a shudder, he shook his head. Maybe it was better this way after all.

A hazy sun struggled to warm the frozen earth as Josiah and his father slid across the snow in the sleigh toward Salem Town. The road was covered in the same deep drifts that kept the family from making the trip in the wagon every Sunday to go to Meeting. As Josiah watched the snow fly up from the sleigh's runners like fine silver filings, he wished the Hutchinsons had a sleigh.

But no. If it meant being like the Porters, he'd rather walk everywhere.

"Are you having a conversation with yourself?" Papa asked.

"Aye, sir."

Papa gave a half smile. "That's why you're able to make such wise decisions. Because you talk things out with yourself—and with God, I hope."

"Aye," Josiah said again.

Papa took his eyes off the horses for a moment and looked at him. They looked even bluer than usual against his red-cold skin.

"I am proud of you, son," he said. "You have been honest with me, and I know I don't always make that easy. I have had to learn to trust my children—ever since the incident of the gold chain with your sister last summer."

Josiah nodded.

"But honesty isn't just keeping your tongue from lying, you know. It also means telling the complete truth. Do you understand?"

Josiah nodded again, sadly. He did understand. He'd said that to Hope, but it hadn't done any good.

"Is there any more of the truth that you want to tell me before we go to court on Monday?" Papa asked.

For a moment, the rest of the story teetered on Josiah's

lips. Perhaps he should tell his father about the Merry Band—about the other people who were there that night.

"I can teach you all I know," his father went on. "In fact, that is what I have tried to do. But I cannot be responsible for your actions—and you have taught me that. Just as you are about to do, each man must deal with God and make his choices on his own in the end."

Josiah clamped his lips together. *The same is true for Hope, William, Ezekiel, and the others,* he thought. *I cannot be responsible for their actions.*

"No, Papa," Josiah said. "I've told you all I need to tell you."

"Good, then," Papa said.

And they drove off into the snow.

Chapter Eighteen

For a while, being at the English mansion in Salem Town almost made Josiah forget about the trial.

"Josiah, you've come home, then!" pretty Mary English sang out as they climbed the front steps to the door. "It's about time you came to your senses and let us have him back," she said to Papa.

The elegant Phillip English stood behind her, leaning on his gold and ivory walking stick and beaming at Josiah. "How is our budding sea captain?" he said.

Josiah couldn't think of anything to say that made sense, so he just nodded.

Phillip nodded with him. "I hear you've run into a bit of rough sailing, eh? Well, not to worry. Salem judges are fair and wise." He winked. "And you have a fine lawyer, too."

Papa chuckled and followed them into the best room, where a tray loaded with all of Josiah's favorite goodies waited for them.

"Cook heard you were coming and made an extra batch of macaroons," Mary said. "Tea, Joseph?"

It was always hard for Josiah to get used to the sparkling presence of Mary English. Unlike his shy, Puritan mother, Mrs. English held her own in male conversations and had even been known to disagree with her husband now and then. Josiah had always thought that Hope would probably be like her someday.

The thought of Hope turned the macaroon to mushy sand in his mouth. Would he ever be friends with his sister again?

But the conversation turned to memories of last summer, and once more Josiah pushed his sad thoughts to the back of his mind where they could rest for a while.

"Would you like a walk down to the harbor this afternoon, Josiah?" Phillip English asked. "It's bitterly cold on the water this time of year, but I don't think that will bother you much if you can see the ships, eh?"

So Josiah had his jaunt to the ships he loved so much, and later a supper by the fire in the Englishs' polished dining room. When he climbed into the high bed he had slept in all summer, he fell asleep at once—and didn't dream of crows at all.

On Sunday morning, they went to Meeting, and Josiah was determined to pray extra hard for the day that lay ahead.

He found a seat on a bench in the gallery where all the boys sat, away from their parents so their boyish pranks wouldn't disturb the serious prayer going on below. But Josiah's prayers were probably the most serious in the church as he bowed his head and squeezed his eyes shut.

Lord, please show me your sacred laws, he began. *And give me a powerful voice—*

He stopped as he felt a nudge at his elbow. He cut a glance to the side and saw Nathan Hollingsworth sitting beside him.

Nathan was the son of Captain Hollingsworth, Phillip English's rival shipowner. He was Mr. English's enemy only by his own choice, Josiah knew, but that didn't stop his overgrown son from bullying any boy who was a friend to Phillip. Josiah had had enough experiences in this very Meeting House last summer to teach him that.

"You're back, then," Nathan hissed. "Who told you that you could sit here?"

Josiah didn't answer and tried to go back to his prayers.

The next nudge was so hard, it made Josiah gasp. He looked at Nathan again, who was glancing over his shoulders to check the location of the tithing man. There was sure to be a deacon close by, looking after the behavior of the boys. If they were caught talking in Meeting, they'd each be popped with the deacon's long pole. Josiah scooted away from Nathan and bent his head again.

Nathan slid with him and once more gave him a jab. This time Josiah brought his head up and looked Nathan squarely in the eye. "Stop it," he said in the loudest voice he dared use.

It didn't escape the notice of the deacon. The tall, thin

man with the scraggly beard and shiny bald head picked his way down the aisle, already waving his pole.

"What is the meaning of this?" he whispered hoarsely when he reached Josiah's row.

Josiah stood up. "I have no idea," he whispered back. "Perhaps you should ask this boy."

He returned to his seat and bowed his head again. Out of the corner of his half-closed eyes, he saw the deacon pull big Nathan Hollingsworth off the bench and drag him by the ear to the gallery steps.

The boy in front of Josiah turned to stare at him and then leaned in to whisper to his friend. "Who is that?" Josiah heard him say as the boy pointed at him.

Josiah wasn't sure he could have answered that question himself. He wasn't certain who he was anymore. He surely wasn't the same boy who had sat in this gallery last summer.

And then he smiled to himself. He wished Ezekiel and William could have seen this.

But that thought made him sad, and he went back to his prayers.

Sunday dinner at the English house was the usual merry affair, and afternoon Meeting was quiet and even comforting. Reverend Higginson's voice was always gentle and reassuring, even if Josiah couldn't remember everything he said in his two-hour sermon.

But even with all of that, Josiah awoke Monday morning with fear pumping through his veins. Breakfast went cold on his plate, and his teeth chattered with more than the chill wind as he and Papa climbed into the sleigh for the ride to the court.

He tried to turn his attention to other things and looked at the buildings they passed in this strange part of town Josiah hadn't visited before.

"What is that building, Papa?" he asked.

"That would be the jail, son."

Josiah groaned and turned his head away. He didn't want to see any bony arms clawing through the bars for help.

To Josiah's surprise, the Town House where Papa halted the sleigh was a small building. Inside, it was plain and dark with only some chairs and a long empty table at the front of the room.

"This is just the Magistrate's Court," Papa whispered to him as they took their seats.

Josiah didn't wonder why his father was whispering. The air of the place was thick with the solemnity of the law.

Just remember that it's the sacred law that matters, Josiah told himself. He made sure his pouch was tied securely around his waist. He had a feeling he would need to be reminded.

A few other people shuffled into the room and took seats. Josiah noticed with relief that none of them were in chains. He thought perhaps this might not be so bad— until he saw Thomas and Nathaniel Putnam enter the room.

His father stiffened, and Josiah's stomach tried to tie itself into yet one more knot. The two men stood in the doorway, letting their eyes grow used to the dim light, and both saw Josiah and his father at once. Nathaniel's big face immediately began to burn red, but Thomas Putnam smiled with forced politeness and nodded to them.

A door at the front of the room opened, and three men dressed in black entered as everyone stood up.

"That is John Hathorne, Jonathon Corwin, and Bartholomew Gedney," Papa whispered.

Why does it take three judges to try me? Josiah thought.

"They are simply magistrates," Papa said, as if that would comfort him. Josiah had no idea what a magistrate was. Papa chuckled softly. "John Hathorne is Israel Porter's brother-in-law. That should make you feel more at ease, eh?"

Josiah didn't answer. It made him feel worse.

John Hathorne rapped on the table where the three magistrates had taken their seats, and a hush fell over the room.

"The first case, please," he said.

A clerk with a bluish nose stood up and read the names from a parchment, but Josiah didn't recognize any of them.

"There are other cases to be heard," Papa whispered. "We must wait our turn."

Jonathon Corwin looked sternly at Papa, and for an awful moment Josiah thought he was going to throw his father in jail for disturbing the court. But John Hathorne leaned over and whispered something to him, and the magistrate smiled faintly and turned his attention back to the case at hand.

For two hours, Josiah sat next to his father in the court-room and tried not to squirm. The magistrates and citizens droned on about which cornfield belonged to whom and who was responsible for the death of a pig one farmer had sold to another. The only thing that kept Josiah from crawling out of his skin was that not a one of them was dragged off to jail. At most, a farmer was asked to pay a large fine for some wrong he had done. But even that made Josiah sink down in his seat. What if his father had to pay their good money for the things he'd done? He tried to sit up straight. He would just have to earn the money himself to pay his father back, that was all. He was responsible, and he would—

"Joseph Hutchinson, you are here accused of the destruction of a fence, owned by one Nathaniel Putnam of Salem Village . . ."

Josiah's head came up, and his heart thundered inside his chest. The clerk was reading from his parchment again, and his father had risen from his chair. Josiah sprang from his own chair and stood beside him. All three magistrates looked at him curiously.

". . . and are also implied in the burning destruction of an outbuilding said to belong to one Thomas Putnam of Salem Village."

"Would those parties aforementioned please approach and be seated here?" John Hathorne said as he flourished his hand grandly toward the empty chairs in the front of the room. His voice was proper and stiff, and it sent chills through Josiah as he followed his father toward the table.

"Mr. Hutchinson, why is your son coming forward?" Jonathon Corwin said.

"Because he is the accused, sir," Papa said. "I am merely here to represent him."

Jonathon Corwin's eyebrows drew together like confused caterpillars. "We allow no lawyers in this court, Mr. Hutchinson."

John Hathorne tapped his fingers on the table for attention. "I think we can make an exception in this case," he said. "The accused is, after all, a boy."

"But I did not accuse *him!*" Thomas Putnam cried. "I accused his father! He must take the responsibility for his son's actions!"

Jonathon Corwin looked down his long, pointy nose at Thomas Putnam. "Who is this man?" he asked.

"You know very well who I am—"

"Thomas Putnam," John Hathorne replied. "He is the person bringing suit against—the Hutchinsons."

"Against *Joseph* Hutchinson!" Thomas shouted. His polite face had gone scarlet, and his angry voice sounded out of place in this room full of quiet, wise people.

"Sit down, Mr. Putnam, before I have you thrown out of this court and your case with you." Magistrate Corwin stared at Thomas Putnam until he sank into his seat, mumbling furiously to himself.

John Hathorne looked up from the parchment and said to his fellow magistrates, "I think I understand Mr. Hutchinson's point. It was his son who supposedly tore down the fence, burned the shed, and so on. While Mr. Putnam thought it appropriate to hold the father responsible, the son wishes to stand up for himself in this." He looked over the parchment at Josiah for the first time. "I think we must applaud that, gentlemen. Perhaps if more of the villagers had done that as children, we would not be seeing so many of them in court now." His eyes shifted to Thomas Putnam. "I move that we proceed."

"Aye," said Jonathon Corwin.

Josiah let out a puff of air. So far the wind was blowing their way. None of the magistrates seemed to like Thomas Putnam very much.

But within minutes, Josiah's heart was again pounding. Whether or not they thought much of the Putnams, these magistrates were out to find the truth.

Thomas Putnam took his place in a chair beside the magistrates' table, which faced the courtroom, and his face was smooth and calm now. He looked at no one but the judges as he waited for their questions.

"Mr. Putnam," said Jonathon Corwin. "What reason do you have to believe that this—boy—is responsible for these charges you and your brother have brought against him?"

"My reason, sir, is that I trust my own son and nephews."

"What do you mean, Mr. Putnam? Please be clear."

"On the night in question, my nephews Silas and Richard saw Josiah Hutchinson leave the shed that later that evening burned down on my property. And my son Jonathon and my nephew Eleazer were witness to the scene when this boy dismantled my brother's fence and dumped the wood on his property."

The magistrates looked at each other and then at Josiah's father with puzzled faces. If he were them, Josiah thought, he'd dismiss the case right now and put him in jail. What could be more proof that he was guilty?

"Why did you not bring your son and nephews here to testify?" John Hathorne asked.

"Because—" Thomas Putnam looked at Papa, "—*I* am willing to stand up for *my* boys."

Josiah heard his father growling under his breath, but he remained in his seat.

"Did they actually see this boy set fire to the shed?" Magistrate Hathorne asked.

"No, but—"

"And did they see him take apart the fence?"

Thomas Putnam smiled triumphantly. "Aye, sir. They did!"

John Hathorne sat back in his seat and looked helplessly at Papa. Josiah felt pretty helpless himself.

"Sir, may I ask a question of Mr. Putnam?" Papa said.

"I will not have him examining me!" Thomas cried.

The magistrates put their heads together, and John Hathorne's came up first.

"Yes, Mr. Hutchinson, since you are your son's representative, you may ask a question."

Thomas's face went purple, and he gripped the arms of the chair until his knuckles turned white. Nervously, Josiah watched his father.

Papa stood up and cleared his throat. "Mr. Putnam, what were your son and nephew doing out that night? Wasn't it a dark, cold winter evening in Salem Village?"

"Aye, but my sister-in-law Marta Putnam heard noises on the property and she sent Jonathon and Eleazer out to see who was about. There is a good deal of thievery and bad dealings goes on in that village, and you know it, Joseph Hutchinson."

"Simply answer the questions, Mr. Putnam," Magistrate Hathorne said.

"And when they reached the fence," Papa went on, "they found that it had been taken down. Did they catch my son, Josiah, in the act?"

"They saw him," Thomas said gruffly, "but when they went after him, he ran. Sure sign that he was guilty, as far as I can see."

"They didn't catch him, though?"

"No!" Thomas cried impatiently. "I've told you that— though they did give him a run for his money, I understand. They had him cornered for some time before they decided it was wiser to come and find us."

"And did they?"

"Aye, just moments later as I returned from the village meeting at Ingersoll's Ordinary."

"Where did you go then?"

"I myself went back to my own home, but Nathaniel—"

"And what did you find when you reached your property?"

"I saw a good deal of smoke, and I found that an outbuilding on the edge of my land had just burned to the ground."

"Can you tell me, Thomas, how it was that my son was

able to both burn down the shed and take down the fence —at the same time precisely?"

"It wasn't the same time!"

"It had to be. You have already told us that your brave son and his cousin had Josiah cornered for some time— too long for him to have completely burnt down the shed by the time you got there—eh?"

John Hathorne was nodding, but Jonathon Corwin still scowled. "I would like to ask the boy some questions," he said.

"Of course." Papa looked grateful to have someone else take over. Although he had made Thomas Putnam's word seem doubtful, he really hadn't proven anything yet.

Thomas Putnam left his seat, still red-faced, and Josiah sank into it. The wood was warm from Thomas's nervous body. Josiah held on to his pouch and could feel the stones through the cloth.

"Boy, you know you must tell the truth—or God have mercy on your soul," Jonathon Corwin said.

"Aye, sir," Josiah said clearly.

"Did you take down the fence that Nathaniel Putnam recently built on his property?"

"I took down a fence, sir," Josiah said. "But it wasn't on his property."

Magistrate Corwin bunched his eyebrows again. "Whose property was it?"

"Benjamin Porter's, sir."

"How do you know it was Porter's land and not Putnam's?"

"My father and his friends said so, and I have naught to do but believe them."

"That was my land!" Nathaniel shouted.

Jonathon Corwin was on him in a flash. "One more outburst from either of you and I will have you expelled from this court. Now, see you keep quiet!"

The Putnams turned their heads like angry schoolboys and Magistrate Corwin went on. "If your father and his friends knew this, why did you not let them handle it as they saw fit?"

Josiah looked down at his pouch. "That would have been the right thing to do, sir," he said. "I wish I had done that. But I thought I was helping the cause of my father and the people he trusts. I know now that I wasn't."

The judge looked stunned as he exchanged glances with his fellow magistrates.

"I think you are correct," Jonathon Corwin said. "You realize, of course, that by admitting your crime, the court will go easier on you."

Does that mean I won't go to jail? Josiah wanted to cry out.

But Papa stood up then, and Josiah looked at him and gasped. Next to him stood Giles Porter, Ezekiel's handsome cousin. His face was ruddy from the cold, and Josiah could only guess that he had just ridden on horseback from Salem Village.

"If I may, sir?" Papa said.

"Yes, Mr. Hutchinson."

"I should like to point out, sir, that my son is correct about one thing."

"What is that, Mr. Hutchinson?"

Papa took a piece of paper from Giles's hand and stepped forward to the table. "The land on which Nathaniel Putnam built the fence does belong to Benjamin Porter."

"You have proof of this, Mr. Hutchinson?"

"Aye," he said. "It took some time to locate, but Israel Porter has procured for me the official record of the deed that he passed on to his son—"

"Israel Porter has a fine way of giving away land that never belonged to him." Thomas Putnam's voice sounded as if it were straining on the end of a leash. "If I may say so, sir."

"You may not," Magistrate Hathorne said. "May I see that, Joseph?"

The document was passed to the table, and the three magistrates bent over it. Josiah looked at his father, his mouth hanging open.

"Giles brought it to me just now," Papa whispered to him. "Israel was good enough to locate it for me."

"Nathaniel Putnam." Jonathon Corwin looked down his nose. "I suggest you withdraw your charge and pray that Benjamin Porter does not bring a similar one on you."

Nathaniel Putnam glowered and snarled and shifted in his seat, but none of the magistrates took their eyes off him. "Let you withdraw it, then," he said finally.

Giles Porter smiled his handsome smile at Papa and quietly left the courtroom.

"But what of my charge?" Thomas Putnam said, his voice growing dangerously close to the shout that would get him tossed from the courtroom. "What of the burning of my shed?"

"I am coming to that, Mr. Putnam," Jonathon Corwin said, "if you will allow me the privilege of conducting my business as I see fit."

"Good, then," Thomas said. "Let you do it."

Once again, Magistrate Corwin turned to Josiah. "Did you burn down the shed that Mr. Putnam refers to?"

"No, sir," he said.

"Have you ever visited this shed?"

"Yes, sir."

"Why? Did you not know it belonged to someone else?"

"I didn't know that, sir. I didn't think it was on Mr. Putnam's property, and it hadn't been used in some time, that was easy to see."

John Hathorne gave a short laugh. "Are we talking about an abandoned building?"

"Aye, sir," Josiah said.

Magistrate Hathorne chuckled into his parchment, but Jonathon Corwin continued to scowl as he said, "Nonetheless, it was not *your* building, and therefore you ran the risk of trespassing on someone else's property."

"Aye, sir. I should have made sure before I went in."

"Did you go in on the night it burned?"

"Aye, sir."

"Before you went to take down the fence?"

"Aye, sir."

"Did you set it on fire?"

"No, sir!"

"Could you have set it on fire—by accident?" John Hathorne put in.

"No—we—I built no fire that night."

While the judge pondered his next question, Josiah bit furiously at his lip. He had almost slipped. Had they noticed? Would the next query be, Did you have anyone with you? He was sworn to honesty. Should he tell on his friends? His stomach tightened, and he put his hand on it to try to calm it down.

"Are you ill, son?" John Hathorne asked.

"No, sir," Josiah said. *Only sick in my heart.*

"Did you see or hear anyone else near the shed before you left?" Jonathon Corwin said.

"Yes!" Josiah said.

"What did you hear?"

"When I was inside the shed, I heard a noise, like something moving outside. But I thought it was only some snow falling from a tree."

John Hathorne looked disappointed.

"When did you first know that the shed had burned down?" Jonathon Corwin said.

"When I returned to it after the Putnam boys chased me. It was already burning then. I tried to put it out myself, but I couldn't."

Jonathon Corwin sat back in his chair and carefully studied his hands. "It seems to me, gentlemen," he said to the magistrates at his sides, "that we have a case here of one person's word against another's." He pointed his long nose at Josiah. "Now, boy, if you know of any other person who saw what you saw, you would be cleared of these charges."

Josiah gasped. It was coming. The question he was dreading was already on Jonathon Corwin's lips.

"Was there anyone else with you that night, young Mr. Hutchinson?" he said. "Is there anyone else who can prove that your story is true?"

Wildly, Josiah looked around the court. But there was no one there to save him. There was nothing. Only the voice of Magistrate Jonathon Corwin saying sharply, "Answer me, boy!"

Chapter Nineteen

Josiah curled his fingers tightly around the pouch. The Indian woman had been there with him. She had probably even seen who started the fire. But he couldn't name her. What was the word of an Indian in such a court? Besides, he would never want her to feel as he did right now—as if she were being squeezed between two boulders.

And Abigail said she knew who had burned down the shed. Ha! She would sit right here in this chair and lie, no matter whom she had promised to tell the truth.

"Josiah, you must answer the question," Papa said quietly.

Josiah took a deep breath. He had made a promise, and he had to keep it. "There was—there was someone with me," he said.

"What does he say? Speak up, boy!"

"He said there was someone with him."

Everyone stared at Bartholomew Gedney, who had scarcely said a word since the trial began.

"And what's more, I believe him," he said. "This is a brave boy. We have seen that. But to have come up with this entire scheme by himself, and to venture out into the bitter cold of the night to carry it out alone—does no one else find that hard to fathom?"

Heads bobbed and then turned once again to Josiah.

"Who was it, then?" Jonathon Corwin said. "Who was there? Who can prove that what you say is true?"

"We can," said a voice in the back of the courtroom.

All heads turned again.

Standing in the doorway were Sarah Proctor, William, and Hope. Nudging them through was Joseph Putnam.

Josiah felt his face drain.

"What in heaven's name?" Papa muttered.

There was confusion in the courtroom as John Hathorne rapped on the table, Jonathon Corwin and Bartholomew Gedney crisscrossed questions to each other, and the Putnams shouted from their seats.

"What is this now?" Thomas Putnam cried.

"You cannot trust this man!" Nathaniel roared. "He will say anything as long as it is against us!"

"Who are these people?" Jonathon Corwin demanded.

The din settled, and Joseph Putnam led the three children to the magistrates' table. Their faces were as pale as porridge, and they clung to each other as if that were the only way they could remain standing. Josiah could only stare at them in disbelief. He didn't dare hope why they were here.

"I am Joseph Putnam," said his teacher. "I have brought the children here because I think they can shed some light on this case. If they may be heard, of course?"

Thomas Putnam stood up, but a look from Magistrate Corwin plunked him back into his chair.

"Anything to clear up this matter, of course," Jonathon Corwin said with a sigh. "You are sworn to tell the truth, as are the children."

"Aye," Joseph Putnam said.

The children nodded timidly.

"Go on, then. Boy, you stay where you are."

Josiah had no intention of moving. He was sure his wobbly legs wouldn't even allow him to stand up.

"I should like to clear Josiah's name first, if I may, Joseph?" young Putnam said to Papa.

Josiah's father nodded. He looked as confused as anyone.

"I have witnesses here, sirs, who will testify that Josiah Hutchinson did not act on his own. One of them was in fact with him at the scene of the fence and the fire."

Magistrate Corwin cut down the line of children with his eyes. "Which of you was it?"

Joseph Putnam looked at William, and for a fleeting moment, Josiah wished he had never brought him. He was certain William was about to throw up right there on the courtroom floor.

But something allowed William to step forward and to say, "It was I, sir. I helped take down the fence. And I was there when the shed burned down. Josiah Hutchinson had naught to do with the fire, sir."

Magistrate Corwin leaned toward him. "Boy, why did you not—"

But John Hathorne put his hand on his arm. "I am not sure this young man can answer any more questions, Jonathon. Perhaps it is enough he has told us this, eh?"

Tears swam in William's pale eyes, and Joseph Putnam drew him back gently. "Thank you, sir," he said to Magistrate Hathorne.

"These girls, then." Jonathon Corwin peered at Sarah and Hope. "Were you with these boys? Did you, too, see the fire?"

Sarah looked as if she would rather die than open her mouth. It was Hope who stepped forward and tilted her chin.

"Sir, I would be happy to answer your questions," she said. "But may I ask that you speak loudly? I am half deaf, you see."

Josiah could barely smother a smile. She was back. The old Hope Hutchinson was back.

"Certainly!" Magistrate Corwin shouted. He looked around uncomfortably and continued. "What is your place in all this foolishness?"

"We didn't think it foolish, sir—"

"Who is 'we'?"

"Josiah and myself, Sarah Proctor and William—" She stopped and looked at Josiah. "We formed a band whose idea was to help our parents in a secret way when there was trouble in the village."

"What kind of trouble?"

Hope looked directly at Nathaniel Putnam. "When Mr. Putnam built a fence on Benjamin Porter's property, that created much ill feeling in the village, sir. We thought to help by removing the fence."

"Did you indeed?"

"I didn't myself, nor did Sarah. But we helped in the planning. We must take responsibility for it as well."

You didn't have to say all of that, Josiah thought. *It was Benjamin's property all along.* But he smiled to himself. He was glad she had.

"And this fire?" Magistrate Corwin said. "Did you see it?"

"No, but I met at the shed with my friends many times. It was our secret meeting place. We would never burn it down!"

"That was not part of this—plan, then?"

"No, sir."

Jonathon Corwin looked at his fellow judges and then directed his gaze at Thomas Putnam.

"We have witnesses who say the boy did not burn down this useless building. Do you have witnesses who will say they did? In a court of law, Mr. Putnam? Under oath?"

Thomas Putnam turned his beet-red face on Hope. "Sir, these are not witnesses! They are children—friends of this boy. They would say anything to support his story!"

"I am not a child," someone said quietly.

Jonathon Corwin looked at Joseph Putnam. "What do you say, sir?"

"I am not a child. Am I to be believed?"

"Certainly," Magistrate Corwin said, "but were you there?"

"No, but I think what I have to say will bring all of this to an end. Let me say first that I am proud of these children for speaking the truth, even if it meant they might be punished. Much has been accomplished here today. As it turns out, they might have gotten off without doing so, but I am happy that they did." He looked at Papa. "I was able to get to the town records, Joseph. Forgive me for not telling you first what I've found, but if I may . . ."

Papa nodded. "Please, Joseph. Go on."

Joseph Putnam reached into his satchel and pulled out a yellowed piece of parchment, which he placed on the magistrates' table.

"This, gentlemen, is the deed to the piece of property on which the building that burned down once sat. You will notice that the land did not belong to Thomas Putnam at all, nor did the abandoned building. It may, of course, have caught your attention that it would be strange for any building in a village the size of Salem to be unused, what with land being so scarce and the space for storage in such demand. Mr. Putnam didn't use the building because he didn't know it was there. It in fact sat on property that Mr. Hutchinson's father donated to the church when he gave the land for the Meeting House." Joseph smiled at Papa. "When your father began to have his own disagreements with the church in Salem Village, he took back some of the land, but he was too bitter ever to do anything with it. It has sat, unowned and unused, for some time." His clear eyes darted to Josiah. "So you see, Captain, that shed was yours as heir to the Hutchinson estate. Perhaps you should file a suit against whoever burned it down."

"You are not suggesting that my son and nephew would do such a thing!" Thomas Putnam cried.

"No," Joseph said quietly. "Are you?"

There was a good deal of shuffling and pushing as Thomas Putnam dove toward his half brother. Papa caught him by one arm and the clerk by the other. Amid much shouting, threatening, and banging of fists, the Putnam brothers were removed from the courtroom.

The magistrates looked at each other in bewilderment. Poor Jonathon Corwin's eyebrows looked to be irreversibly tangled together, he was so confused.

"Well, gentlemen," John Hathorne said finally, "I think we can reasonably consider this case closed."

"Agreed." Bartholomew Gedney dusted his hands off to prove it.

But Jonathon Corwin looked once more down his long, slender nose at the four children gathered in front of him. "Aye," he said. "But let me advise you, boys and girls. See you stay out of the affairs of your parents, lest you get yourselves into trouble no one can pull you out of. Am I clear?"

There was no answer, and Josiah wished desperately that Hope would say something.

"I think they are waiting for your response, sir," Magistrate Corwin said.

"I, sir?" Josiah glanced at his friends. All three of them had their eyes glued on him—eyes that said, *Please answer for us. You're the leader.*

"Agreed, sir," Josiah said in a clear voice. "I can promise you that."

And then he sighed from the bottom of his toes. There wasn't a doubt in his mind that he would keep that promise.

Chapter Twenty

ever in Massachusetts history was there a sleigh ride like the one they took back to Salem Village that afternoon, Josiah decided.

Wrapped in blankets, he, Hope, Sarah, and William huddled together in the sleigh, their cheeks glowing bright red from the cold—and from happiness.

"What made you come?" Josiah shouted as Papa drove the horses through the snow.

"You did, Josiah!" Hope cried.

"I?"

"Yes! You told me to go to Joseph Putnam and I did. When he told me about the crow, I knew I couldn't leave you to take all the responsibility yourself. I don't know how I ever thought I could."

"Not that you needed our help." Sarah smiled shyly. "You were so brave in there. I couldn't even speak!"

"But how did you come to be there, too?" Josiah asked.

William poked him from his other side. "When I saw Hope talking to Joseph, I couldn't stand it anymore. I didn't care whether Papa beat me into a piece of boot leather—I had to come."

"And did he whip you?" Josiah said.

"No!" Sarah said. "He told us it is a brave thing to admit when you're wrong. Almost the bravest thing a person can do."

Papa turned from the horses and frowned at them. "Why must you children think we fathers are such monsters? Our only wish is to see you raised to be fine people." Then he smiled. "And that you are. All of you."

Josiah grinned at his friends. They were a fine Merry Band. All except two.

Josiah's doubts about the Porters crowded back into his mind. Israel Porter would lend them a sleigh to make the journey, and send his grandson with a document to help prove his innocence, and even tell his brother-in-law the judge to make things easy for them. But he would never stand beside them himself. And Ezekiel and Rachel, it seemed, were the same way.

But thoughts of Ezekiel and Rachel would have to wait until later. For now, there was celebrating to do. And Papa had the perfect idea.

"I think there must be cider and popcorn at the Proctor Inn, eh?" he said over his shoulder.

Everyone squealed—Josiah the loudest.

The shadowy thoughts of Ezekiel didn't return until several days later when Josiah was walking home from school late in the afternoon. He had just left Joseph's house when something made him look back. From out of the trees flew Ezekiel, tearing toward Joseph's front door.

Josiah didn't shout to him, but instead ran after him, his boots digging furiously into the snow. Ezekiel tried to get away, but Josiah was faster and quickly had him straddled on the ground.

"Don't hit me!" Ezekiel cried. "Don't—please!"

"I wasn't going to hit you," Josiah said. "I only want to talk to you."

"You can't hold me, Josiah Hutchinson. I've a message to deliver to Joseph for my grandfather."

"And you shall do it, when I'm finished," Josiah said.

Ezekiel sulked. "What is it, then?"

"I have a gift for you."

The sulk froze as all understanding drained from Ezekiel's face. "A gift?"

"Aye."

"You want to give me a gift after . . . I didn't go to my father to tell on you, you know! I went to tell him that the Putnams were on our land!" He stopped and bit his lip. "What sort of gift?" he said. "A snake down my back?"

Josiah snorted. "A snake? In winter? Some scout you are, Ezekiel Porter!" He chuckled again as he reached into his pouch and pressed a stone into Ezekiel's hand.

"What is it?"

"It's to remind you to have some sense and act by what

you know is right," Josiah said. "When you do that, maybe we can be friends again."

With that, he stood up and left Ezekiel lying in the snow, staring at the stone.

"What is it?" he called after Josiah.

"It's a crow!" he shouted back. "Ask Joseph Putnam about it!"

Ezekiel was still gazing at it as Josiah disappeared into the trees.

He hadn't gone but a few feet when he heard someone whisper, "Boy!"

Josiah stopped and looked around. A blue shawl poked out from between the trees. Josiah grinned.

"Indian woman!"

She didn't smile, but brushed past him to peer at Ezekiel, still lying in the snow.

"It's all right," Josiah said. "He wasn't going to hurt me."

She nodded, but he could see she wasn't convinced.

"Wife of Wolf." He felt suddenly shy, but there was something he had to say. "Thank you for the gifts you've given me. They've—they've helped me remember things I'd forgotten."

She nodded happily.

"I—I wish I had a gift for you."

She shook her head.

"No. You've given me a lot, and I haven't given you anything. I even—I even bothered you about Oneko, and I know you don't want to talk about him." He shrugged. "That's all I wanted to say."

Slowly, she reached out her hand and placed it on his chest. "Good," she said.

This time Josiah watched her as she slipped away.

Although the trial had cleared the cobwebs from Josiah's life, it wasn't the cure for all of his father's worries, or Joseph Putnam's. His father still walked around with anxious lines etching his face, and Josiah often saw Joseph Putnam staring out the window of the classroom when he and William were working quietly. That night, he found out why.

In spite of the need to conserve firewood, when Joseph Putnam came to their house after supper, Papa took him into the best room. Josiah was sent in with firewood and then with a tray of corn cakes and cider. When he entered the room with the second load of wood, the men did not stop talking. Josiah worked slowly and listened.

"I want you to know, Joseph," Joseph Putnam said, "that although you have decided to stay with Israel Porter and see this thing through, I do not begrudge you that. I simply cannot remain a part of it any longer."

"And I envy you your ability to make your decision," Papa said. "I, on the other hand, continue to waver back and forth like a baby's cradle. One day I think Israel Porter the wisest man in Massachusetts. I think his plan for us to all return to Salem Village Church and try to right it from the inside, taking over the church ourselves, to be the only answer."

"And then," Papa went on, "I wonder if that be not too harsh. Reverend Parris tries, I know it. He came here and prayed over my daughter when she was dying. They say he goes into the jail and prays with the prisoners. He is no demon, that's sure. I understand he dotes on his own daughter, just as I do on my children." He shook his head. "I need more time to know what is right."

"There is no fault in that," Joseph said. "Perhaps I have made my choice too quickly. It's sure it has cost me a friend and a student. Just today Israel sent me a message declaring that if I remain at odds with this plan, our unborn baby will receive no part of his estate when he dies."

Josiah dropped a log. Unborn baby? Constance was— she was going to have a baby? This was surely a conversation worth listening to!

"He would deny his own great-grandchild an inheritance over this difference of opinion?" Papa shook his head sadly. "The children are already too much affected by this. We must settle it, Joseph, before they take it into the next generation."

"Aye," Joseph said, "and I know you will decide what is the best way to do that. But let us not cease to be friends over it, eh?"

There was a silence, and Josiah looked up to see them clasping hands.

"Come here, Josiah," Papa said. "Let you join hands with us in a promise that you will not allow God's people to be divided as we have. That you will try your best to see that it does not happen in your generation."

"Aye, sir," Josiah said. And two pairs of big men's hands swallowed his up in a promise.

When Joseph Putnam was gone, Papa put out the fire in the best room and then looked thoughtfully at Josiah. "I have a mind to go for a walk," he said. "Get your jacket if you want to come along."

Minutes later, they were walking in marching steps through the deep snow. Papa led the way, and to Josiah's surprise, they stopped on the spot where the hideout had burned down. New snow had covered the charred ground, but Papa seemed to know the spot well.

"This was indeed part of my father's land when he first came to Salem Village from Plymouth," Papa said. "I had forgotten about this spot after he gave it away to the church." He chuckled softly. "And then took it back. Hope puts me in mind of your grandfather sometimes. Hotheaded, he was. But I remember this spot now."

"Was it something special?" Josiah asked.

"Aye. He called it the Blessing Place. It was here that he first asked for God's blessing on the land so that his children and grandchildren would prosper here. It was a fine gift to us, that blessing."

"Aye," Josiah said.

It was a peaceful moment, and Josiah closed his eyes and prayed that it would last forever. But he didn't pray quickly enough, for Papa suddenly burst out with an "Ach!" It was his favorite expression when things were in a knot.

"There are extremes in men, Josiah," he said. "Some, like Joseph Putnam, are spotlessly devoted to the truth. Others, like Thomas Putnam, are so coldly self-righteous, you would think ice water ran in their veins. Some, like you, fight for the truth. Others, like the Putnam boys, can only abuse those who do. We all know it was they who burned your cabin down, eh, when they saw you leave it that night? Just for spite." He sighed deeply. "But most of us, son—most of us fall in the center somewhere. Most of us are simply human."

Josiah looked at his father with his tired face lined in worry and pain. How many times had Papa said the right things that had taken those lines out of his own face? Josiah sighed, too. He surely had no answers.

But as if moved by God Himself, Josiah's fingers brushed against his whistle pouch, which dangled below his jacket. With frozen fingers, he opened it and pulled out the wolf stone.

"I have a gift for you, Papa," he said.

Papa's eyebrows went up. "A gift?"

"Aye. It was given to me—by an Indian friend. It isn't a good luck charm or—or any such nonsense. It is just a reminder that—" Josiah stopped, suddenly afraid Papa wouldn't understand.

"Go on," his father said.

"It is just a reminder that perhaps you should be the one to teach your friends what's right—because you probably already know what is."

Timidly, he tucked the wolf stone into his father's hand and watched as he brought it close to his eyes to see it in the darkness. He stared at it for a long time before he looked at his son. "Thank you, Josiah. I shall keep it always."

The next day after supper, four shadowy figures appeared at the base of Hawthorne's Hill on a patch of ground where the snow covered their burned memories. The sun shone amber on its whiteness as the four huddled together, shivering but smiling.

"We found your message tucked beneath some logs in our woodshed!" William said through his chattering teeth.

"We hoped you'd find it," said Hope.

"What is this meeting about?" Sarah said carefully. "I know we got away with our last plan without punishment, but I—"

"It's nothing like that," Hope assured her. "Josiah, tell them."

All eyes turned to Josiah as he spoke. "We are a Merry Band that should always be together," he told them. "We proved that in the courtroom, did we not?"

They all nodded.

"But being a Merry Band does not mean we have to take part in a war, does it?"

William shook his head slowly. "No. But what else is there to do?"

"Good deeds," Josiah said. "Things that will teach these—"

"Stiff-necked people," Hope put in. "That's what Papa calls them."

"Aye. That will teach these stiff-necked people what goodness really is."

"Do you have any ideas, Josiah?" Sarah asked.

Josiah shook his head. "Not yet. But we shall think of something, eh?"

"Aye!" Hope said. "After all, we are the Merry Band!"

They all clasped hands and shouted together in the middle of the Blessing Place. Josiah shouted, too, and felt only a little bit sad that Ezekiel and Rachel weren't with them. There would be time to teach them, too. He knew there would be.

It was nearly dark as Hope and Josiah headed back toward the Hutchinson farm. Hope was chatting happily about the meeting when Josiah thought he heard a thin whistle from far behind the parsonage. Hope, of course, didn't hear it.

"I should like to spend a minute by myself," Josiah said to her.

"Why?"

"I don't know—just to think."

Hope looked at him closely. "You are becoming a strange boy, Josiah. But all right. Don't freeze, now."

"I won't." He watched her tromp on through the snow. When she turned the bend, he dashed down the hill behind the parsonage and pulled out his own whistle. His signal was rewarded with another. It had to be the Indian woman, or maybe William with something he'd forgotten to say— or even Ezekiel asking for forgiveness. Josiah searched eagerly into the darkness. But the figure who emerged from the trees was none of those. The boy who suddenly appeared before him was a tall Indian boy.

Josiah could barely speak. "Oneko!"

From behind him, Wife of Wolf also appeared. She looked

around uneasily and put her hand on Oneko's arm.

"Your father doesn't know you're here, does he?" Josiah said.

Oneko shook his head.

But beyond that, Josiah couldn't say anything else. He could only look at his friend, whom he hadn't seen for so long. Oneko had grown tall, and he looked so much older than Josiah. Even his face was tight with the cares of someone much advanced in years.

"Can we be friends again?" Josiah said finally. "Is that what this means?"

There was no answer. They only looked at him.

"No," Josiah spoke for them.

Oneko looked down at the Indian woman and said something to her in a clipped but polite tone. She cocked her head and slowly nodded, but before she backed away, she shook her finger at him. It was in that minute that Josiah knew. She was Oneko's mother.

She took a few steps back until she was hidden watchfully behind a tree. Josiah moved toward Oneko, but the Indian pulled back, almost the way a wolf would do if a human tried to get too close.

"It's me, Oneko!" Josiah said. "You know I won't hurt you."

Oneko shook his head.

"It isn't me you're afraid of, is it?" Josiah said.

Again, Oneko said no with his eyes.

"Is it your father?"

Their eyes met and Josiah knew he was right. Oneko's father hated the white man. He had made that clear the one time Josiah had met him. It was such a stupid hate. One that kept Josiah apart from the best friend he had ever had.

But Josiah knew more about hate now, and so he nodded. "I understand," he said. "I'm not angry with you."

At last Oneko smiled. Josiah's face broke into a grin, too. Seeing that look on Oneko's face again, like the sun rising in it, would last a long time in his memory.

A hissing came from the bushes and Oneko turned toward it. Wife of Wolf motioned for him to come.

"Go!" Josiah whispered. "Don't get into trouble for me."

Oneko hesitated for only a moment before he turned and slipped away with his mother. As he watched them disappear into the trees, Josiah wished again that he had a gift for them.

And then he remembered something. "God bless you," he called out softly.

Because he knew now that God's blessing was the finest gift anyone could give.

1. Lt. John Putnam
2. Widow's Cabin
3. Joseph Putnam
4. Sgt. Putnam
5. Capt. Walcott
6. Rev. Parris
7. Meeting House
8. Nathan Ingersoll
9. Nathaniel Putnam
10. Israel Porter
11. Dr. Griggs
12. John Porter's Mill
13. John & Elizabeth
    Proctor

A Map of
SALEM VILLAGE
& Vicinity in 1692

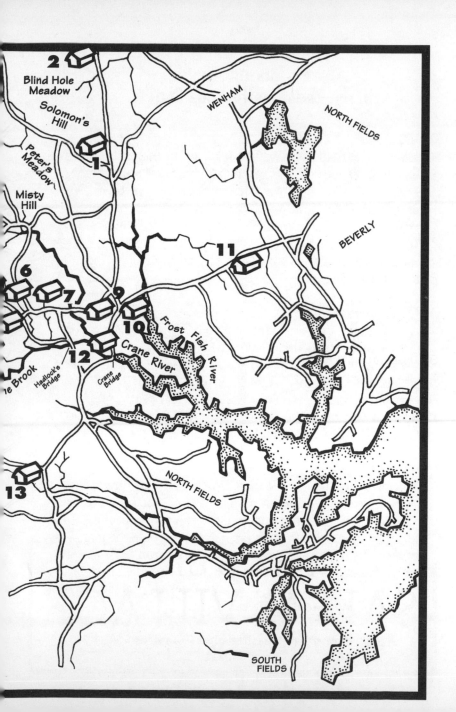

There's More Adventure in the Christian Heritage Series!

The Rescue #1

Josiah had wished there was no Hope in his life! But that was before the accident, when he and his older sister, Hope, fought a lot. Now, she's very sick. And neither the town doctor nor all the family's wishing can save her. Their only earthly chance is an old widow —a stranger to Salem Village—whose very presence could destroy the family's relationship with everyone else! Can she save Hope? And at what price?

The Stowaway #2

Josiah is going to town! Sent to Salem Town to be educated, Josiah Hutchinson's dream of someday becoming a sailor now seems within reach, and nothing is going to stop him . . . or so he thinks! A tough orphan named Simon has other plans, and his evil schemes could get both Josiah and Hope in a heap of trouble. How will the kids prove their innocence? Whose story will the village believe?

The Guardian #3

The wolves are in Salem Village! Josiah has heard them howling at night. Although many of the neighbors set traps to catch them, Josiah has devised a better way of dealing with them. But with the perfect night to execute the plan approaching, there's still one not-so-small problem— Cousin Rebecca—who follows Josiah around like his shadow . . . even into danger! How will Josiah protect her? What will happen to the wolves?

Available at a fine Christian bookstore near you.

Focus on the Family Publications

Focus on the Family

This complimentary magazine provides inspiring stories, thought-provoking articles and helpful information for families interested in traditional, biblical values. Each issue also includes a "Focus on the Family" radio broadcast schedule.

Brio

Designed especially for teen girls, *Brio* is packed with super stories, intriguing interviews and amusing articles on the topics they care about most—relationships, fitness, fashion and more—all from a Christian perspective.

Breakaway

With colorful graphics, hot topics and humor, this magazine for teen guys helps them keep their faith on course and gives the latest info on sports, music, celebrities . . . even girls. Best of all, this publication shows teens how they can put their Christian faith into practice and resist peer pressure.

All magazines are published monthly except where otherwise noted. For more information regarding these and other resources, please call Focus on the Family at (719) 531-5181, or write to us at Focus on the Family, Colorado Springs, CO 80995.